John G Gittings

Personal Recollections of Stonewall Jackson

Also Sketches and Stories

John G Gittings

Personal Recollections of Stonewall Jackson
Also Sketches and Stories

ISBN/EAN: 9783337065478

Printed in Europe, USA, Canada, Australia, Japan

Cover: Foto ©Andreas Hilbeck / pixelio.de

More available books at **www.hansebooks.com**

Personal Recollections

 ## of Stonewall Jackson,

—ALSO—

SKETCHES AND STORIES.

BY
JOHN G. GITTINGS.

CINCINNATI.
THE EDITOR PUBLISHING COMPANY.
1899.

CONTENTS.

PERSONAL RECOLLECTIONS

OF

"STONEWALL JACKSON."

PART I.

STONEWALL JACKSON.

PERSONAL RECOLLECTIONS OF "STONEWALL" JACKSON.

BY JOHN G. GITTINGS.

(Late Adjutant 31st. Virginia Infantry and Major
Confederate Cavalry).

PART I.

Major Thomas Jonathan Jackson was a professor at the Virginia Military Institute, at Lexington, Virginia, when the writer, a cadet, first met him in the year 1852.

A relative of Jackson and coming from his native town, he bore a letter of introdution to him, which letter, however, was not presented; for this young recruit had met with such a warm reception from the older cadets on his arrival, and was withal, so depressed by the rigid discipline of the school, that he feared to face this professor, whom he looked upon even then as a hero, one who had received the "baptism of fire" in Mexico, and was "the only officer promoted twice in one day"—as he had been informed by the village chronicler, who thus dilated on the

1

achievements of Jackson in the war against the Mexicans.

I found on my arrival at the school that Jackson was then absent and would not return for some weeks; in fact, I had been a cadet for a month before I finally met him.

One evening shortly after his return, he sent the sergeant of the guard with the order that I should report at his quarters without delay. On receiving this order my first thought was that I had violated some one of the innumerable military rules and was about to be called to an account therefor; so it was with some trepidation that I went to the Major's quarters.

However, he met me at the door of his room with a pleasant smile; he took my cap and placed it carefully on the table, gave me the best chair, then seating himself, began to look on me critically, as if taking an inventory of my person. He spoke kindly of our mutual friends, in quick, sharp and rather inarticulate tones, and appeared to be making an effort at politeness: but boy as I was, I thought his manner strained and awkward, yet I regarded him with deference, and perhaps awe.

This was my first meeting with "Stonewall" Jackson. He was then about twenty-eight years of age, six feet tall, with gray-blue eyes, a well chiseled aquiline nose, and a very fair and ruddy countenance. He wore side whiskers, and one noting his complexion, ruddy countenance, and reserved manner, might have mistaken him for an Englishman; but here the resemblance ceased, for in thought and expression, this quiet, unaffected man was all American.

As I sat in his presence that day, and observed his diffidence, this thought passed through my mind: Can this modest man be the one who fought so bravely in Mexico; and who stood by his cannon after all his men had been killed or driven away?

* * * * *

Thomas Jonathan Jackson, the subject of this sketch, was born in the town of Clarksburg, now West Virginia, on the 21st of January, 1824. His birthplace was a little story-and-a-half brick house which stood on Main Street nearly opposite the court house. This building was torn down only a few years since. His father, who was a lawyer of good ability, died when "Tom" was only three years old, leaving his widowed mother with his sister Julia, an infant in arms, together with his brother, Warren, perhaps two years older than himself. The father's grave is still to be seen, marked by a simple head-stone, in the old "Jackson graveyard" at the eastern end of town. The young widow and her children were left almost destitute, but they had a large family connection of Jacksons in this vicinity, and among them the children and their

mother lived for several years, until the time
when the mother remarried and the elder
brother, Warren, had died. "Tom" was then
left to the care of his uncle, Cummins Jackson,
and grew up at "Jackson's mills," sixteen miles
south of Clarksburg. Here he received the
little schooling the country could afford, and,
at least could read and write. He did chores
about the mill and also acted as a deputy sheriff
of Lewis County, until about the age of eighteen,
when he learned of the vacancy at West Point,
from this congressional district.

Cummins Jackson, a rugged, stern man, was
very kind to his young relative, and let him
have his own way pretty much. He was a man
of ample means, and lived with a free hand;
he kept race horses, and was fond of sport generally. Little Tom was noted as being almost a
sure winner whenever he rode his uncle's racers,
which he did on important occasions.

The writer has been told by men who knew
him that Cummins Jackson was a fine speciman
of physical manhood. They said he was a
giant in stature and built in proportion.

The fact is that "Stonewall" Jackson was descended from a long line of distinguished
ancestry, men prominent in the affairs of this
section, both in state and nation, from before
the Revolution down to the present day.

The family had its rise from the union of

John Jackson and Elizabeth Cummins, emigrants from England, who came over in the same ship in the year 1748. Soon after their arrival in this country they were married in Maryland. They then removed to the vicinity of Moorfield, Hardy County. In the year 1765 they crossed the Alleghany mountains and settled in the wilderness on the Buckhannon River, near a place afterwards known as Jackson's Fort, but which is now the town of Buckhannon.

John Jackson was of Scotch Irish descent; he was about twenty-three years of age when he crossed the ocean to make his home in the western wilderness. He has been described as "a man of medium stature, of great goodness, industry, and tranquil courage."

Elizabeth Cummins, the young English girl who united her fortune with his, and from whom the Jacksons are said to have derived their vigor of body and intellect, had a romantic history. She was the daughter of a landlord in London; her father was the proprietor of a public house called "THE BOLD DRAGOON." As the name would indicate, the place was the resort of the military officers of the garrisons near by. Elizabeth is described to have been a stately blonde, nearly six feet in stature, and almost perfect in form and feature. She was well educated and possessed a resolute, active mind. It happened on a day when she was about sixteen years of age, that a soldier, presumably an officer, offered her some impertinence, or what she considered as such, and which excited the ire of the stately beauty, till in her anger she hurled a heavy tankard at his head with such force that it laid him bleeding and senseless on the floor.

In her fright at what she had done, she hastily left the house and repaired to the docks, where she took refuge on a vessel that was just weighing anchor, bound for America. She was acquainted with the captain of the ship, and also made friends with a family who was glad to have her accompany them to the colony of Lord Baltimore in Maryland. Thus she met her future husband, and left England never to return.

They lived in the western wilderness, in the turmoil of the Indian warfare, until the breaking out of the Revolutionary struggle. Meanwhile, they had acquired some of the most valuable real estate in this section of the country, and had each of them played their part in the hand to hand conflicts with the savages.

It is the tradition, that on an occasion when an Indian had killed a white man near the˝settlement, while the rest of the men were at work at a distance, Elizabeth Jackson took down her husband's rifle, and calling the dogs, chased the savage out of the neighborhood before the men could be collected.

On the breaking out of the Revolutionary war John Jackson and his elder sons, George and Edward, the latter the grandfather of "Stonewall," bore their part as soldiers, staunch and true, and at the close returned to their homes in the wilds of Virginia.

Col. George Jackson, who lived at Clarksburg, became a member of the First Congress under the Constitution, and Edward Jackson also became a member of a later Congress.

One of the most distinguished members of the family was John G. Jackson of Clarksburg, where many of his descendents still reside. He was the eldest son of George Jackson, and served in Congress for about twenty years, and finally became the Federal Judge of the Western District of Virginia, which office he held until his death in 1825. It was in this year that the mother of the family, Elizabeth Cummins Jackson, died, at the great age of one hundred and five years! Her husband had died twenty-four years before, at the age of eighty-six.

Judge John G. Jackson, before there was any outlet from this region save by pack-horses over the mountains, built iron forges and furnaces, woollen-mills, foundries, and salt-wells; he proposed to make the West Fork river navigable for steam-boats, by building slack water dams; and also, by a short tunnel, he would turn the head waters of the Buckhannon river into the

West Fork and thus increase its volume of water.   And as before the clearing of the forest
along the head streams, the volume of water
was much more constant than at present, and
with the supply, by tunnel, from the Buckhannon river, men now say his plan was feasible,
and all this he would probably have accomplished seventy years ago, had not death strick-
en him down, at the early age of forty-seven
years!

Lately, surveys of the West Fork of the Mo-
nongahela river have been ordered by the
National Congress, and a liberal appropriation
for that purpose has been made, in order to
make this river navigable, and to carry out the
designs that Judge Jackson had put in active
operation nearly three quarters of a century
ago.   But now that the river banks have been
denuded, to a great extent, of their forests; and
that the hydrographic conditions have entirely
changed, it is believed that it is now impracti-
cable to make this channel navigable for any except small boats.

In connection with this family history, it may
be stated that the first wife of Judge John G.
Jackson was a sister of Dolly Madison, the wife
of the President.   They were married in the
White House during its occupancy by President
Madison, and it is said that this was the
first marriage that was ever celebrated in that

historic building.   Judge Jackson's second wife
was Mary Meigs the daughter of Return Jonathan Meigs, Governor of Ohio. Governor Meigs
was a son of that Colonel Return Jonathan
Meigs   of   the Revolutionary   army,   who
marched through the wilderness of Maine, as a
colonel of Connecticut militia, with Benedict
Arnold to the siege of Quebec.   He was by the
side of Montgomery, when that gallant officer
fell in the assault on the Citadel. Meigs served
with great distinction, to the close of the eight
years' struggle for liberty.   He received a vote
from the Continental Congress thanking him
for having captured a British fleet at Sackett's
Harbor; that body also presented him with a
handsome sword in acknowledgment of his services to his country.

"Stonewall" Jackson always took a lively interest in his family history; and from Mrs.
Jackson's Memoirs of her husband, and to
which work we are indebted, we learn that prior
to the war he wrote to his cousin William L.
Jackson, then Lieutenant Governor of Virginia,
in behalf of some relative who was running for
a political office. W. L. Jackson afterwards
served on the staff of "Stonewall" in the war;
he subsequently became a general, in command of a cavalry brigade; he survived the war,
and after serving as a judge for many years, in
Kentucky, lately died at Louisville.

In the letter above alluded to, "Stonewall"
wrote to his cousin : "I am most anxious to see
our family enjoying that high standard and
influence which it possessed in days of yore."

He said his Jackson relations were "very
clannish" and he was warm in his family attach-
ments, himself. But he would give none of
them military office, unless they first proved
themselves worthy of it, by actual service on
the battle-field. From this section, he appointed
his relative Col. Alfred H. Jackson on his staff.
This gallant officer fell on the battle-field of Cedar Mountain and died soon thereafter. He was
buried in the cemetery at Lexington near
"Stone-wall's" grave.

"Stonewall's" mother was Julia Neale, the
daughter of Thomas Neale, of Parkersburg ; her
father was descended on the maternal side from
the Lewises, a distinguished family, the relatives of Washington, and prominent in the Indian wars and Revolutionary history.

"Stonewall" Jackson felt all the pride of descent from a long line of worthy ancestors; he
also felt his lack of education and how much it
would cripple him in his efforts to rise from the
humble position in which he had been cast by
cruel fate.

Hence, while he was riding over the hills of
Lewis County, in the performance of his duties
as deputy sheriff, when the news was brought to

him that there was a vacancy at West Point from his congressional district, he immediately set about to obtain the appointment. His friends, knowing his manly, brave spirit, and knowing also, that it was of such metal that soldiers were made, were especially anxious that he should obtain the appointment.

Tom now began to study his books at night, after his hard labor of the day. He was doubtful about his ability to enter West Point, but was determined that he would fail through no lack of effort on his part, either to obtain the appointment, or to sustain himself after he had done so. But his impetuous temper could not brook delay; so it came about that he started alone, and with poor outfit, on the long journey to Washington City before he had received any notice that he could get the appointment!

*   *   *   *   *

The writer lives in the town where Jackson was born, and has often conversed with old citizens who were men grown at that time; they have told him that Jackson made the journey on foot to Washington, a distance of nearly three hundred miles—carrying his clothing in his saddle-bags—in order to solicit the appointment to West Point from Mr. Hays, the representative from this district.

It is said Mr. Hays was much startled at the apparition of a country boy, dressed in homespun and all travel stained, marching into his presence, with saddle-pockets on his shoulder and abruptly demanding the appointment as a cadet to West Point!

The congressman thought that, considering his limited opportunities, surely Jackson was not qualified to pass the examination which was required to enter that institution. But when he had learned that he had made the long journey on foot, over two mountain ranges and through the forest, for three hundred miles, merely to ask for the appointment, and that "he must have it," then he replied: "You shall have it!"

It is related that after Mr. Hays had consented to give him the appointment, he asked Jackson if he would not like to walk over the city and see the sights, but he declined, saying, "he would like to climb up in the dome of the Capitol and take a view from there, and then he would be ready to go on to West Point and begin his work, and he was anxious to do so as soon as possible."

His life at West Point was a long struggle : he was barely able to sustain himself in his class for a year or two, but he gradually forged ahead, and it was thought that if the course of study had been several years longer, he would have climbed to the top. The cadets, at first, were disposed to treat him with especial rigor, as he appeared unsophistocated, but in time they came to respect him and to believe that with his sin-

cerity of purpose, and unwearied application, he
would be able to acquit himself with credit, which
he did.

     *   *   *   *   *

Let us return now, to the scenes at the Virginia
Military Institute, and to my intercourse with
Jackson as a professor before I knew him in the
sterner duties of war.

It was not until my second year at the Military Academy that I came to recite in the classes
taught by Major Jackson, but in the meanwhile
I was under his instruction at artillery practice,
which consisted principally, as far as the
"plebes" were concerned, in drawing the pieces
and caissons.

Jackson always wore his uniform and his military cap, the visor of which almost touched his
nose; he was lank and long-limbed and walked
with a long, measured stride, swaying his arms
leisurely, while his gray-blue eyes seemed to
search the ground in front. His brow was ex-
pressive and bore, without doubt, the impress of
genius. "Calm dignity; unaffected modesty;
sincerity; and the intense honesty of his nature
were imprinted on his countenance," and shown
forth in every trait of his manners.

I will admit that the cadets generally, did not
regard him in this light, but differently; yet
such was my opinion at the time, and in looking
back through the vista of years, I believe it to be
a correct one.

At the artillery practice we soon learned that Major Jackson was a very strict and exacting officer. He expected every cannoneer to do his duty, and every "plebe", who served in place of a horse, too!

One day on the parade ground a fellow "plebe" managed, in some way, to draw out a linchpin from the wheel of a "limber" at which I was pulling, and as a consequence, in trotting down hill at a fast pace, the wheel flew off with considerable force. As the fates would have it, it rolled directly towards "Old Jack," who was looking in an opposite direction. He turned his head in time to see its approach, and although it passed within a few inches of his person, he did not budge from his tracks.

A cadet remarked: "He would not have moved if it had been a cannon ball going right through him!" But we soon observed that his gaze was fixed intently on our battery in a way that made us feel very uncomfortable, and in a brief space we were placed under arrest—officers, cannoneers, horses, all; and as a result this breach of discipline was settled in a way that did not invite any repetition of the offense.

Professor Jackson was an able instructor at artillery tactics, but in the regular collegiate course he did not appear to have any special genius for teaching; yet he was always a conscientious, laborious instructor. He was said to be dyspeptic, and perhaps was something of a hypochondriac, as his health had been very much impaired by his service in Mexico; he had been at a water-cure establishment in the north, and the prescription had been given him to live on stale bread and buttermilk. He followed this prescription for some time while boarding in the hotel in Lexington, and these peculiarities attracted the attention of the public and he was much laughed at by the rude and coarse. He bore all their jests with patience. In a like manner he carried out another order from the water-cure—to go to bed at nine o'clock. If that hour found him at a party, a lecture, or a religious exercise, he would invariably take his leave. His dyspepsia caused drowsiness and he often went to sleep while sitting in his chair; he was a devout member of the Presbyterian church, over which the Rev. Dr. White presided, but he would sleep during the service. And it is stated that Jackson was thrown into confusion, on a public occasion, when a mesmerist failed to put him to sleep—some one in the audience called out—"No one can put Major Jackson to sleep but Rev. Dr. White!"

It was the custom at the Military School to fire salutes of artillery on the Fourth of July and Washington's birthday. In honor of such occasions Major Jackson would always don his best uniform and wear his finest sword, a very handsome one, which the cadets said had been presented to him by the ladies of New Orleans at the close of the Mexican War.

In the gray dawn of the morning he would come marching on the parade ground, with his fine sabre tucked well up under his left arm. He had the long stride, as has been noticed, like that of a dismounted cavalryman, and on such occasions his manners would be brisk, if not cheery, for he took special pride in these celebrations and was very punctilious in all their observances.

Major Jackson married a daughter of Doctor Junkin, president of Washington College, in the second year of my stay at Lexington. He then took up his residence in the town. Before his removal from the barracks, however, an incident occurred which will go to show the estimate in which he was held, even by the most intractable characters. A number of cadets who were about to be dismissed through incompetency in their studies or for excess of demerit marks, while on a Christmas frolic made a raid on the professors' rooms in the barracks, and despoiled them. Major Jackson's room alone was left intact. It is difficult to determine why these young vandals should have respected his quarters when they seemed to respect nothing else. Some suggested that as cadets, they respected his military fame won in Mexico. It is a notable fact that even at

BIRTHPLACE OF STONEWALL JACKSON.

that time the cadets had an abiding faith in
Jackson as a military man, and perhaps very
few of them were ever afterwards much surprised
at his great achievements in war.

But I have learned that after my time at the
institute, Jackson became unpopular as a professor through his rigid notions of discipline,
and his uncompromising enforcement of the
rules. He was intolerant of neglect of duty,
inattention to studies, and carelessness at drill
and thereby became uncongenial, and through
his eccentricities became an object of the tricks
and witticisms of idle cadets.

*   *   *   *   *

He was one of the most scrupulously truthful
men that ever lived, and even carried his exact-
itude of expression and performance to extremes
in small matters.

On one occasion he borrowed the key of the
library of one of the literary societies, and
promised the secretary to return it within an
hour. However, becoming absorbed in his book,
he put the key in his pocket and did not think
of it again until he had reached his boarding
place, in the town, nearly a mile away. Then,
although a hard storm had sprung up in the
meantime, he turned about and marched all the
way back through the rain to deliver the key as
he had promised, though he knew the library

would not be used and the key would not be needed on that day.

In conversation if he ever happened to make an ironical remark, even if it were so plainly ironical that none could misapprehend it, yet would he invariably qualify his expression by saying: "Not meaning exactly what I say." This peculiarity of speech became almost a by-word with the cadets and subjected him to much embarrassment, but such was his regard for truth that he would not depart from it, even in e st, without immediately correcting his statement.

He belonged to a literary society in Lexington which embraced in its membership men of learning and ability. It was a custom of the society to hold a series of public lectures during the winter season. This was one of the few entertainments the cadets were permitted to attend, and when Major Jackson's turn came to lecture there was considerable interest evinced by them, in anticipating the subject of his lecture, and the manner in which he would acquit himself.

When he appeared on the lecture platform, he was embarrassed, it is true, and his lecture lacked in oratorical effect; yet it was said at the time to have been one of the best of the whole course, and was very entertaining. The subject of his discourse was "Acoustics," and he discussed very effectively all that was then known about the properties of sound. He said that it was "an undeveloped science," and that no doubt in the near future progress would be made in it, and discoveries, especially in the "transmission of sound." This prediction has since been verified in the perfecting of the telephone. * * * It must be admitted that Major Jackson was regarded by the cadets and others as an eccentric man; either from his impaired health by his service in Mexico, or from some other cause, it remains a fact, that he always seemed to be more or less sensitive and ill at ease in his intercourse with strangers.

Speaking from a social standpoint, no man ever had a more delicate regard for the feelings of others than he, and nothing would embarrass him more than any *contretemps* that might occur in his presence, to cause pain or distress of mind to others. Hence he was truly a polite man, and while his manner was often constrained and even awkward, yet he would usually make a favorable impression through his evident desire to please. However, before he became famous in war, he was generally underrated by his casual acquaintances, for in such society he was a taciturn man, and would listen in silence, while others discoursed at length upon subjects in which he was himself well versed. He would thus create a false impression of his own acquirements, which were very considerable outside of collegiate learning, and embraced a wide knowledge of men and things.

*   *   *   *   *

About the second year of my stay at the Virginia Military Institute, Major Jackson was suffering from weak eyes and he would not read by artificial light. So, when near one of the examinations our class had prevailed on him to give us a review of a difficult study, he was compelled to hear us after dark, the only time he had to spare for the purpose. We used to meet in the "section room" in the dark. Professor Jackson sat in front of us on his platform, and with closed eyes questioned us over many pages of a complicated study. This work required a strong effort of memory and concentration of thought, and no doubt it was just such exercise that fitted him for his duties in the field—in holding in his mental grasp the countless details that perplex the mind of a commander of armies.

*   *   *   *   *

It was one of the marked characteristics of Major Jackson that he always inspired confidence in those who knew him intimately. The cadets believed in him as a religious man, although, as has been stated, he would sit placidly and sleep through a greater part of the long, tedious sermons of the Presbyterian divine in whose church he was an elder. They knew that he slept because of physical weakness, and that insincerity was not a part of his nature.

Governor Letcher, of Virginia, who had been familiar with him for a number of years, appointed him to a colonelcy at the beginning of the war, and he never had a doubt of Jackson's capacity to fill any rank in the army, however great.

Major Jackson was married twice; he lost his first wife while the writer was still at the Military Institute. The Rev. Dr. White, the aged minister of the Presbyterian Church, officiated at the funeral, to which the cadets marched as a guard of honor. After the services were over at the grave and the attendants had all left the ground except the cadets who were forming their ranks at a distance, it was noticed that Jackson was standing alone with uncovered head by the open grave, as one distraught. The venerable clergyman, who was a lame man, was compelled to hobble all the way back from the gate and lead him away, as he would heed none other.

In the year 1857, after having returned from a tour of Europe, Major Jackson was united in marriage to Miss Anna Morrison, the daughter of a Presbyterian minister of Lincoln County, North Carolina. His widow still survives him; by this marriage there was one child, a daughter, Julia, who lived to womanhood and married

a Mr. Christian. This daughter died, leaving
two children, a son and daughter, as the only
lineal descendants of "Stonewall" Jackson.

Mrs. Jackson, the widow of the General, has
written an interesting life of her husband, which
dwells especially upon his charming home life
and religious character.

*   *   *   *

Soon after the outbreak of war, the writer
was ordered to Harper's Ferry to see General
Jackson on military business, and arrived at his
office about daybreak, on a morning in May.
This was his regular office hour when he received
the reports of his subordinate officers; and after
hearing the reports of the officer of the day, the
officer of the guard, scouts, and others, he would
dispatch business in a very prompt and ener-
getic way. He knew exactly what ought to be
done and how it should be done. There was no
wavering in opinion, no doubts and misgivings;
his orders were clear and decisive. It occurred
to us at the time that Jackson was much more
in his element here, as an army officer, than when
in the professor's chair at Lexington. It seemed
that the sights and sounds of war had aroused
his energies; his manner had become brusque
and imperative; his face was bronzed from exposure, his beard was now of no formal style,
but was worn unshorn.

What sort of a man is this? They were surely

but shallow judges of men who mistook Jackson
for a fool; yet there were such, who set him
down as an ill-balanced professor out of his
groove, and they thought it unsafe to put thousands of men under his command. This was re-
peated when he was made a colonel; it was reiterated when he was made a brigadier, and a major-general, and a lieutenant-general. The fact
of the matter is, that there were men, even at
the beginning of the war, who felt assured that
Jackson was capable of any command; and his
career illustrates the justice of this judgment,
for great as were his commands and mighty as
were the thunderbolts of war which he hurled
against opposing columns, he never had a command that overtaxed his abilities. It is impossible to judge of the limitations of a personality
so unique, or of a force so tremendous as was
concentrated in the military genius of this officer—had he only a force at his command equal
to the full measure of his capacity. Napoleon
has said that it was difficult for him to find
among all his generals one who could command
a division of ten thousand men and handle them
as they ought to be maneuvered in a campaign.

It is the opinion of the writer, who served under Jackson throughout his career, that he
would have been more successful as commander-
in-chief than he was as lieutenant-general; his
military character was different from that of

any other general. If he ever devised any complicated theory of a campaign, he kept it in his
own head. The fact is he never divulged his
plans; he was always on the ground to direct
for himself; he knew the topography of the
country in which he carried on his campaigns
as well as the people who lived there. The old
inhabitants of a section were often surprised
when Jackson informed them of roads and paths
through their country which were forgotten,
or unknown to them.

He had his engineer officers plot in their
charts every natural feature of the region
about his army, and he absorbed it all from their
drawings or from actual inspection. He knew
every ravine, water-course, bridle-path, and
blind-road of the country in which he carried
on his operations. The plans of most generals
consist of many complicated parts, and although
concocted with consummate ability, some of them
are sure to fail in the day of battle; for it is impossible to strike as with one blow, and at the same
instant, from many different points. The strategy of Jackson's plans never failed; all his wonderful feats were accomplished by rapid marching; so that the rest of the army used to call our
command "Jackson's foot-cavalry." He would
concentrate his forces by rapid movements, day
and night, and strike at an unexpected point,
like a thunderbolt. It is singular to consider

that while the Union generals knew that Jackson was as swift as the wind, and were always making plans that they might guard against this, yet he continued to the end of his career to take them by surprise, by swinging his forces around their flanks, and doubling up the wings of their columns and lines of battle, when they had thought he was still serving with his command in a distant field. * * *

And now, thirty-five years after the death of Jackson, we can write of his campaigns dispassionately, since the northern and the southern soldier have mingled their blood on battle fields, in bearing to victory the "Stars and Strips," on a foreign soil.

And Confederate veterans indorse the sentiments of their heroic commander, General John B. Gordon, when three years ago from the rostrum in Baltimore, he held forth his hand and said:

"I extend this old right hand of mine and pledge its eternal defense of the glorious flag of the Union, the flag of Washington and Jefferson and Franklin, that now waves over this united country." And how true has come his prophecy—"And wherever that flag shall wave, there will it find the loyal sons of the South rallying to its support, willing to shed their blood and to lay down their lives to make it the symbol of freedom and equality and brotherhood."

The memorable deeds of arms, on both sides

of the line, in the Civil war, must remain forever, as a glorious record of the courage and manhood of the American soldier.

Swayed by such sentiment, the victorious legions of General Grant's army, at Appomattox, drew up in line and presented arms to the starving, ragged remnant of the Confederate forces, as they marched by to lay down the guns they had wielded with intrepidity for four years.

"The bravest are the tenderest," and the manly feeling in the breasts of Grant's veterans paid this voluntary tribute of courtesy and honor, to the broken ranks of a valorous army, overwhelmed and borne down by numbers.

It was a tradition in the army, that while Jackson was stationed at Harper's Ferry, a stranger, a man of middle age, was observed walking through the camp. He fell in conversation with the soldiers and asked the name of the commanding officer. When told that Colonel Jackson of the Military School at Lexington was in command, he said: "O yes, I know him: and I tell you men, if this war lasts any time, Jackson will be heard from!" and he continued, "I wouldn't be surprised to hear that Jackson is the commander-in-chief before the war is over!"

The recruits were greatly surprised and also pleased at this high praise of their commanding officer, from a stranger who seemed to have such unbounded confidence in him. But it was thought afterwards that this stranger had served with Jackson in Mexico.

When the writer visited Jackson's camp at Harper's Ferry in May 1861, he was at that time busily engaged in organizing and drilling his troops. He said he was unable to send any of his regiments as requested to the relief of Colonel Porterfield in Northwestern Virginia; that it must be represented to that officer that he himself was in a situation of great danger, as there was a force of the enemy within a day's march of him, that greatly exceeded his own command. He expressed a deep interest in the Northwest, as it was his native section, and he always afterwards evinced the same interest in that part of the state. Indeed, it was his desire that he might be sent there in command; but as a soldier, he served where ordered without complaint.

General Joseph E. Johnson now assumed command in the Valley Department, and in the early encounters along the Potomac, which were skirmishes. Jackson attracted his favorable notice, and was appointed a brigadier-general on the third of July. But he first attracted public attention, and even became famous, by the part he bore in the battle of First Manassas; or as it is commonly called "Bull Run."

* * * * *

We shall now recount briefly, the military campaigns of General Jackson, touching alone

the main features of his brilliant achievements.

Bull Run is a small stream, twenty miles long,
forming the boundary line between the counties
of Fairfax and Prince William, in Virginia. The
stream runs in a south-easterly direction and falls
into the Occoquan, a tributary of the Potomac,
about twenty-five miles from Washington City.
The turnpike from Centerville, running west-
ward, crosses the only bridge over Bull Run
within ten miles of the battlefield. But other
available crossing places for troops are the fords
which are to be found at intervals of two or
three miles, up and down the stream.

Upon the banks of this stream was fought the
first important battle of the Civil War, June 21,
1861. General McDowell, commanding the Union
forces in front of Washington, leaving General
Runyon with five thousand men to guard his communications with the rear, advanced with thirty-five thousand troops of all arms, to attack
General Beauregard, who had twenty thousand
Confederates posted for eight miles along the
west side of Bull Run. Gen. Joseph E. Johnston
with about eighteen thousand men was stationed
at Winchester, fifty miles northwest, where he
was watched by General Patterson with about
an equal number.

General Johnston, learning of the advance,
hastened with eleven thousand men to reinforce

Beauregard, while the rest of his army remained
to confront Patterson. The day before the battle
Johnston reached Manassas with six thousand
men, the remainder to come up the next day,
when part did arrive about two o'clock in the
afternoon.

Before daybreak on the twenty-first of July
McDowell sent Burnside's division to cross the
stream above, to move down on the west side,
turn the Confederate left, and clear the bridge
which was defended by an abatis, in order to
cross the remainder of his troops.

This movement was successful; Burnside
was checked only for a short time, on the high
ground at Young's branch, a brook which falls
into Bull Run. But here, reinforced by Sykes'
regulars and the brigades of Sherman and Por-
ter, he drove the Confederates in confusion almost to the edge of the plateau.

It was now noon; the bridge was taken, and
McDowell could cross all the troops he needed.
The battle was practically lost to the Confederates; seven-thousand of them were falling back
in confusion before the advancing eighteen-thou-
sand directed by McDowell. At this juncture,
Jackson with five regiments was advancing in
the center, while the whole Confederate left-wing
was hurled back upon him. Among the latter
troops was the South Carolina Brigade, commanded by General Bee. That officer rode up

to Jackson's Brigade and shouted: "General, they're beating us back!" Jackson replied, sternly: "Then we will give them the bayonet!" This inspired General Bee: he rode back to his troops, and with his drawn sword pointed, exclaimed: "Rally men, on the Virginians! There stands Jackson like a stone wall!"

They did rally on the Virginians, but their heroic commander fell among the slain; yet, with his dying breath, he had christened Jackson and his Brigade with the fame and name of "Stonewall," which lives in history.

This check given to McDowell's victorious advance by Jackson, enabled Johnston and Beauregard to hasten up all their available reinforcements, which after a desperate engagement of several hours, turned the tide of battle, and resulted in the rout of Bull Run.

*   *   *   *   *

Jackson said, the sobriquet, "Stonewall," was won in battle by his brigade, and that it did not belong to him, but should be applied to the "Stonewall Brigade," which consisted of the Second, Fourth, Fifth, Twenty-seventh, and Thirty-third regiments of Virginia Volunteer Infantry.

From the prominent part he had taken in the battle of Manassas, Jackson was promoted to the rank of major-general on the 7th of October; and several weeks thereafter, he was ordered to proceed to Winchester to take command in the Valley of Virginia.

And now he must part with "his brave old Brigade." They were drawn up in line, and in a brief speech he feelingly reviewed the brilliant achievements of these regiments, and bade them an affectionate farewell. But they were not to be long separated, for a few weeks later they were again assigned to his command and served under him until he fell at Chancellorsville.

*   *   *   *   *

On the first day of January 1862, Jackson having been joined at Winchester by General Loring's brigade, and having then under his command about eight thousand five hundred men, projected an expedition against Romney, and other posts in the South Branch Valley.

The weather was mild when his troops marched out of Winchester, but the following day it suddenly changed to be very severe, and with the sleet and snow, the roads became almost impassable. His supply trains were unable to keep up with the moving column, and for several nights his men were compelled to bivouac in the open air, and endured great suffering.

There was a conflict of authority between Jackson and Loring, and although Jackson succeeded in gaining possession temporarily of

Romney and the Valley, without great loss in the skirmishes that followed, nevertheless, the enterprise was generally considered a failure.

General Jackson with his own immediate command fell back to Winchester, but left General Loring with the greater part of the force, in winter quarters near Romney. General Loring protested to the War Department that his situation was hazardous and unnecessary and demanded that he be returned to Winchester. Jackson received an order from the Secretary of War directing him to withdraw Loring's brigade to Winchester. This order he promptly complied with; but he immediately sent his own resignation to the Secretary, saying:

"With such interference with my command, I cannot expect to be of much service in the field!"

But there was such a howl of protest from the public, at the thought of losing the services of Jackson, that the Secretary was alarmed; and through the intercession of General Johnston and Govenor Letcher of Virginia, Jackson was induced to withdraw his resignation. After this, his military operations in the field were never directed from the War office in Richmond!

  *   *   *   *   *

At Kerntown on the 23rd of March 1862, General Jackson attacked a superior force under

General Shields. The action commenced about 3 p. m. and lasted until dark. His men fought desperately, but were compelled to fall back, under the attack of the heavy columns that were hurled against him. This is said to have been the only instance in which "Stonewall" Jackson was ever repulsed. But long afterwards, when the war was over, the writer remembers to have heard General Shields, in a speech at Independence, Missouri, make this remark: "It has been said, that I am the only officer who ever whipped Stonewall Jackson! Now I have only this to say, if I am the only officer who ever whipped old Stonewall—he was never whipped at all!"

This was the testimony of General James Shields, who after receiving a bullet through the lungs, in fighting for the flag in Mexico, lived to fight for the Union, if it may be, still more gallantly in the Civil War.

*   *   *   *   *

In the early part of May, and at the beginning of Jackson's Valley campaign which has been called the most brilliant of the whole war, the positions of the Confederate forces were as follows:

General Edward Johnson with about thirty-five hundred men was at West View, seven miles west of Staunton. This command on the 13th of December 1861, had fought and won a decisive

battle on the top of the Alleghany mountains, but
had moved to its present position, to be in touch
of reinforcements. General Jackson to the astonishment of all, now suddenly appeared in
Staunton with his immediate command of six
thousand men. General Ewell, with an equal
number was hastening from near Gordonsville,
to take Jackson's place at Swift Run Gap, in order to threaten the flank and rear of General
Bank's main command, which was stationed at
Harrisonburg. General Milroy, with the advance of General Fremont's corps, six thousand
strong, was hastening to attack Johnson's feeble
force and thus capture Staunton : while Fremont
with eighteen thousand men was moving up the
South Branch to Milroy's aid.

The rapid and devious movement of Jackson's
troops mystified every one, both friend and
foe; it was impossible to conjecture his plans.
Behind the screen of his cavalry, he would move
his infantry twenty-five or thirty miles a day,
often marching far into the night. Thus, throughout this campaign the position of his army was
not determinable; it might be here, it might be
there, or it might be a hundred miles away!

He gave his troops a rest of one day in Staunton, then continuing his march, joined Johnson's force, drove in Milroy's pickets and for-
aging parties, and camped twenty-five miles
west, on the turnpike. The next morning he

hastened forward Johnson's brigade which took possession on Sitlington's Hill, a position that commanded the village of McDowell, and the camp of Milroy's forces. Following more deliberately with the main body, Jackson deployed a sufficient force, which by making a detour, would be able to gain the road in the rear of the enemy, by midnight.

On the afternoon of this day, May 8th, Milroy attacked in force, the position occupied by Johnson's brigade. The latter, reinforced by a regiment from Jackson's command, repulsed every assault made upon it, though the battle raged fiercely, until after nightfall. The loss was severe on both sides. The full moon arose and looked down on the ghastly scene, on the mountain top; Johnson, the wounded commander of the Confederates was carried from the field. But the battle ceased not, until the whole front of the ridge occupied by the 12th Georgia and 31st Va. regiments (the part of the field of which we can speak from observation) was strewn with the slain.

General Milroy, suspecting a flank movement to his rear, sometime after dark withdrew. He left his camp fires burning brightly, which deceived the confederates, but in the morning his whole force had vanished. He marched all night and reached Franklin in Pendleton County, twenty-four miles distant, where early in the day he met the whole of Fremont's command advancing.

Jackson followed rapidly Milroy's retreat to that place, but after coming up with him and discovering the reinforcement, he did not think it prudent to join battle.

He turned aside, and rested his troops for a day in a pleasant valley; here religious services were held to give thanks for the victory won at McDowell. The soldiers, long after, would recur to this scene; the valley, through which ran a sparkling stream, was inclosed by lofty hills, and clothed in the verdure of Spring. Services were held in nearly every regiment, and Jackson and his staff officers joined in the devotions. * * *

* * *Jackson, uninterrupted by Fremont, continued his march, and in ten days following, covered a distance of one hundeed and ten miles. This brought him to Front Royal, in Warren County, and within eighty-four miles of Washington City. Here on the 23rd of May, he attacked the federal forces, capturing a large amount of stores and gaining possession of the bridge near by, over the Shenandoah. He had now turned the flank and was threatening the communications of Banks' large army at Strasburg. The latter hastily retreated to Winchester.

At Front Royal, Jackson's army rested for a

few hours; next day, marching forward it debouched into the valley pike at Middletown, in the midst of the stragglers and trains of Banks' retreat. Capturing everything at hand, he pressed forward, and in the afternoon came up with the rear-guard of the main command, which was driven before him all that night.

The next morning, the 25th of May, Banks' army, hastily drawn up in line of battle at Winchester, was attacked by Jackson's advance. The resistance at first was determined, but Jackson's regiments, as fast as they arrived on the scene, engaged in the action. Soon, Banks' lines were broken; his brigades and regiments were disorganized, and thrown back in wild confusion. Then began the race for the Potomac, the confederates following in not much better order, but flushed and elated with the joy of victory.

The people of Winchester were zealous in their attachment to the South, and were wrought up with excitment, as the confederate troops raced through their streets, in pursuit of Banks   The ladies, in their enthusiasm, ran from the houses, bearing platters and baskets of biscuits, sweet-cakes and flowers; also pitchers of water—a grateful boon to the over-heated, dust-choked infantry. It was a scene never to be forgotten.

Banks' army was reformed on the north side of the Potomac. Jackson, after the pursuit of a few miles, rested his exhausted troops at Winchester. In the brief space of two days, he had driven Banks' army a distance of fifty miles or more, from Front Royal and Strasburg to the Potomac. The results of the victory were great, and should have been greater, but the cavalry in pursuit were unable to resist the temptations of the spoils of war, that appealed so invitingly to the overworked horsemen, all along the way; thus it happened they were not on hand at the critical moment, when Banks' lines were broken.

Jackson captured here, three-thousand prisoners; also immense wagon-trains laden with quartermaster, commissary, ordnance and medical stores.

The afternoon of the day following was given to religious services in the camp, in returning thanks for the victory. The third day Jackson marched down to Harper's Ferry and bombarded Bank's forces across the Potomac. The alarm had been sounded in Washington and this movement increased the panic.

Although Jackson had now only about fifteen thousand men for duty, the federal forces were hurried from all sides, to intercept his march to the capital.

McClellan was ordered to stop for the present his operations in front of Richmond, and dispatch twenty-thousand men for the Shenandoah. Fremont, Shields and Banks were all gathering their forces and hurrying forward with the same purpose.

After the victory at Winchester, Jackson did in fact appeal to the authorities at Richmond, that his command might be increased to forty-thousand men, with which he proposed to move on Washington. But the request was not granted.

The writer was near the spot, where Jackson was personally directing the operations of a battery which was firing on Banks across the Potomac. A courier rode up in hot haste, bearing a dispatch from Ashby, the tenor of which we could only judge from what occurred afterwards. Jackson very deliberately ordered the battery to "cease firing and limber up." The brigade of infantry which was resting on the road side, was directed to begin its return march up the valley.

This retrograde movement was begun with the usual expedition of 'Jackson's foot cavalry'; when our brigade came to the Capon Springs road, and had turned aside, and marched along it for a mile or so, we met the advance of Fremonts army. We became hotly engaged, and so continued to harass their march, and to hold in check their column, until Jackson's main command had passed up the valley pike.

Sending forward his prisoners and captured trains, laden with all the munitions of war, Jackson marched sixty miles in three days, when he arrived at Strasburg, the key to the situation. Here, he passed out from between the converging lines of three armies that were bearing down upon him. His cavalry had burned the bridges on the lower Shenandoah and Shields was thus compelled to continue his march up the east bank.

Jackson reached Harrisonburg on the 5th of June; here he changed his course and marched towards Port Republic. Fremont was following close after, apparently anxious to give battle. The skirmishing between his advance and Ashby's cavalry was continuous; and that lamented officer fell on the 6th of June, while leading a charge near Cross Keys. Jackson, in his official report, in writing of Ashby, said :"As a partisan officer, I never knew his superior." Leaving Ewell's divison, only eight thousand strong, on the ridge at Cross Keys to resist the advance of Fremont's eighteen thousand, Jackson hastened to Port Republic with the remainder of his small force, and planted his cannon on the heights commanding the bridge, the only approach available for Shields.

On the 8th of June, Fremont attacked Ewell's division at Cross Keys in force; but despite the disparity of numbers, the latter held his ground all that day, and at night withdrew, and by daylight had united his command with that of Jackson at the bridge of Port Republic. Cross-

ing with his united force, Jackson attacked, at
nine o'clock, Shield's army, three-thousand
strong, advancing on that side. It was defeated
and driven back with heavy loss. At this juncture, Fremont with his whole force appeared
on the opposite bank, but the bridge was then
in flames and he made no attempt to cross.

Jackson rested his troops in camp the next
day, but Fremont and Shields retiring from the
conflict, retreated down the valley.

The Confederates then moved out into the
beautiful valley near Weyer's Cave where they
encamped and services were held, returning thanks
for victories won. Thus ended the Valley Campaign of 1862. With a force never exceeding
sixteen thousand, Jackson had for months foiled
and held in check the corps commanded by Mc
Dowell, Fremont, Banks and Shields.

Great as were the achievements of Jackson
in his subsequent, brief career, his after deeds
could scarcely augment the renown he had won
in the Valley Campaign. His surprisingly ag-
gressive movements, the daring of his strategy,
marked by the prevision and forecast of events
that enabled him often to circumvent the enemy,
were his characteristics. Military experts now
began to rate him as an executive officer almost
without a peer among his contemporaries.

*   *   *   *   *

At the close of Jackson's valley campaign,

General McClellan was drawing his lines about Richmond. General Lee who was now in command, resolved to concentrate his forces and to take the initiative in an attack, as Richmond, on account of the lack of supplies, was not in a condition to withstand a siege. In order to mask the movement of Jackson from the valley, several thousand troops were sent, with considerable display, to reinforce him.

Jackson left his camp near Mt. Meridian on the 17th of June; but his destination was unknown even to the men of his command, until he appeared at Ashland, on the evening of the 25th inst. The next day he passed around the right flank of McClellan's army at Mechanicsville, and on the 27th at Gaines' Mills drove his right wing back upon the center, capturing camps, military stores, and many prisoners. Here a federal captain who was captured with his company, and not knowing that Jackson's men were his captors, said to us:

"Well boys you've got the best of us to-day, but you haven't heard the news from Jackson in the valley; his whole command has been broken up! I was reading about it in the New York paper, just as you fellows charged into our camp!"

When the captain had learned the facts in the case, he was dumb with astonishment.

In the bloody "seven days battle" around

Richmond, Jackson's Corps bore a conspicuous part; however, he was not now in independent command, but was subject to the orders of his chief, and was only one of many.

After the battles were over, Jackson's command camped for a few days near Richmond; on the next Sunday he attended services at one of the Presbyterian churches in the city; but he was not known to the citizens by sight, and attracted no special attention.

However, they were annoyed, when they had learned from a soldier, that the officer on a rear seat was the famous "Stonewall" who had come and gone unnoticed of them.

*   *   *   *   *

The return march now began towards the Valley and on the 19th of July Jackson's Corps to reached Gordonsville. His soldiers were glad to breathe again the mountain air: but hundreds of their comrades had fallen in the "seven days battles," in the swamps of the Chickahominy.

A few days later the camp was moved into the county of Louisa, near by, where the troops were recuperated somewhat by a quiet rest. But this was not to last, for General Pope, now in command of the federal forces in this department, was assembling at Culpepper Courthouse and uniting in one body the commands that had fought against Jackson in the Valley. He had in all more than fifty thousand men, and declared by proclamation that "his head-quarters would be in his saddle."

Jackson was reinforced by the division of A. P. Hill and did not await the onset from Pope, but moved against him, and the 9th of August they joined battle at Cedar Mountain. It was late in the afternoon of that day, before the engagement became general. Pope was repulsed, but at the beginning of the battle Jackson contended against great odds and his left wing was swung back; this, however, he quickly re-established by reinforcements coming up. A charge of federal cavalry also bore down in gallant style upon this wing, but they were dispersed with great loss, by the steady fire of artillery and infantry. Darkness closed the bloody drama. Pope, according to his reports, had about thirty-two thousand men engaged in this battle, while Jackson's forces were at least ten thousand less; but the latter had seized the mountain heights where he had planted his cannon and occupied an almost impregnable position. The confederates captured four hundred prisoners, including one general, and fifteen hundred small-arms and other ordnance stores.

On the thirteenth of August, Lee began the movement of his army, from in front of Richmond, to the vicinity of Gordonsville; McClellan was evacuating the peninsula, and removing his troops to the Potomac.

Pope withdrew his command to the north side of the Rappahannock; Jackson, in the advance of Lee, skirmished for several days with his lines, along the upper waters of that river. Then, when the main body was well up to the front, Jackson made a detour with his corps and Stuart's cavalry in order to gain the rear of the enemy. He marched fifty miles in two days and struck Pope's lines at Bristow and Manassas Junction, capturing or destroying the main supplies of his army, and immense stores of the quartermaster and commissary departments fell into his hands. There was sharp fighting at both places, and Jackson captured several hundred prisoners. His presence in the rear of the enemy was now known, and his army occupied a position of extreme peril; his safety lay in falling back upon Thoroughfare Gap, and awaiting reinforcements from Longstreet. He moved first towards Centerville, and then turning west marched a mile beyond the old battlefield of Manassas where he found, in the abandoned railroad cuts, excellent fortifications made to hand. Posting his men behind these, he was attacked by Pope in force, but was soon reinforced by Longstreet, and here began the bloody battle of Second Manassas, which was waged for two days and resulted in the defeat of Pope's army.

On the night of September 2nd, Jackson made

a reconnoisance in force, as far as Ox Hill near Chantilly where an encounter took place, in which the Union generals, Stevens and Kearney, were killed. This was within twenty miles of Washington City, and the authorities were so apprehensive of an attack upon the capital, that the whole army was withdrawn behind the fortifications of the city. * * * * *

General Lee now proposed to invade Maryland. Jackson's corps, on September 5th forded the Potomac at White's Ferry and after destroying the navigation of the canal by breaking the lock-gates, continued its march to Frederick City. Lee, with the whole command, joined it here, four days later.

The graphic incident which gave rise to the poem of "Barbara Frietchie" was said to have occurred on Jackson's entrance into the city. But now it is known there was no occurrence of the kind, for "Barbara Frietchie", the principal actor in the scene, was then ninety-six years old, bed-ridden, and unable to wave a flag; and besides, Jackson's march did not lead him past her residence. Nevertheless, the poem is a beautiful one, and will live.

The large Union forces still left in the vicinity of Harper's Ferry threatened Lee's communications, and Jackson's corps was directed against that place. He left Frederick, September 10th, and by rapid marches by the way of Martinsburg, reached there, and invested that fortification, within four days.

With great effort, Jackson succeeded in planting artillery on the surrounding heights; and on the 15th inst, after a furious bombardment, the garrison was compelled to surrender. Jackson captured, besides the garrison stores and armament, eleven thousand prisoners of war.

Lee, in the meantime, had withdrawn his army from Frederick, on the approach of the whole Union army, under McClellan, who had been reinstated in chief command. He fell back to Sharpsburg, behind the Antietam Creek, ten miles north of Harper's Ferry, where in a strong position, he awaited the attack of McClellan.

This was necessary as his army was greatly reduced; thousands of his men were left along the way, worn out through privation of rest and food. Many were without shoes, and could not keep up in the long marches over the stony roads. General Lee estimated that his army had been reduced to forty thousand men.

Jackson leaving a small guard at Harper's Ferry, with orders to parole the prisoners he had captured there, hastened to rejoin Lee. He arrived on the field about noon of the 16th inst., in time to take part in resisting the assault made against the left wing.

The next day, September 17, 1862, has been called "the bloodiest day in American history;"

for then was fought the great battle of Antietam.

At daybreak, Hooker's corps opened the battle by a furious assault directed against Lee's left wing. Jackson's veterans were here, borne back for nearly half a mile before this fearful onset; but receiving reinforcements, he again advanced, sweeping before him Hooker's and Mansfield's corps, regaining the ground he had lost. The gallant veteran, Mansfield, here fell.

Thus with wavering fortunes, the battle raged throughout the day. Night ended the conflict with both armies concentrated and confronting each other on the west side of the Antietam.

On the 18th the armies maintained a truce to bury the dead. McClellan during the day received large reinforcements, and it was said he purposed to renew the engagement the next day. By that time, Lee had withdrawn across the Potomac. * * *

* * *Jackson's corps rested near Bunker Hill, twelve miles below Winchester, for several weeks. A needed respite for his war-worn veterans, who were really destitute of most of the appointments of a well-equipped army; even clothing and shoes were scarce.

While in this camp near Winchester, Jackson received his last promotion, on the 11th of November. In about eighteen months he had arisen from the rank of colonel, to that of lieutenant-general.

Burnside was now placed in command of the Union Army and immediately began the advance on Fredericksburg, on the Rappahannock. Lee hastened to confront him, and took position on the river hills. Jackson's command marched from Winchester to rejoin Lee, and reached his position near the center of his lines not far from Hamilton's crossing, within eight days. He was compelled to halt and rest his men for two days, as some of them were without shoes.

Jackson's corps was encamped here for about two weeks before the battle.

Burnside's plan as developed, was to cross by three pontoon-bridges near Fredericksburg and three more at a point about three miles below. The construction of these bridges was interfered with somewhat, by the sharp-shooters; but it was no part of Lee's plan to prevent the crossing.

The night preceding the battle was consumed by Jackson's troops in moving up from their camp, several miles below; we, however, had an hour of rest before forming our line of battle. Our position was midway between Fredericksburg and the right of the lines, with a wide extent of plain in front.

It was perhaps, as late as nine o'clock on the 13th before the fog rolled back and revealed Burnside's forces in position on the south side. His lines extended along the first and second

benches of the river bottom, while in front were
planted his numberless field batteries.

This stern array—a hundred thousand strong,
deployed in three lines of battle, of two ranks
each—now marched forward in stately pomp,
with banners waving and bands playing.   Then
the heavy siege guns thundered from the Stafford heights, sending shot and shell, plowing our ranks; while the great columns of
the reserves crowded the passageways to the
bridges. *   *   *
*   *   * Never before had we looked on a
panorama of battle so wide and unobstructed by
forests as this view on the field of Fredericksburg; and as we gazed on the mighty host
marching into action, we felt the scene awe-in-
spiring in its terrible grandeur.

In this engagement Jackson's command was
advanced beyond its position in the line of battle to a point where our lines had been pene-
trated by Mead's Corps. Here the fighting was
stubborn and long continued, but Jackson's men
sustaining their great reputation, finally succeeded in regaining the lost ground, and in re-es-
tablishing the line, but at the cost of many lives.

Burnside's forces were repulsed at all points;
he made the most determined assaults against
Marye's Heights, which was Lee's strongest
position; here, whole brigades were destroyed in
the reckless charges.

The battle was fought on Saturday, and on Sunday the armies lay quiet, each awaiting the attack of the other. On Monday there was a truce to care for the wounded and bury the dead. That night, under the cover of darkness and storm, Burnside withdrew across the river and removed his pontoons.

Thus ended the Virginia campaign of 1862. * * *

* * * Jackson's command went into winter quarters along the Rappahannock and did picket duty as far down as Port Royal; his headquarters were at Moss Neck, about eleven miles below Fredericksburg. Here he occupied a small office in which he was engaged nearly all winter in making out official reports of his battles, and in directing the various duties in regard to supplies, discipline, and the recruiting of his corps. He was busy, but was sometimes interrupted in his work by visits of personal friends whom he always received kindly and with scrupulous politeness. Occasionally a foreign officer called to pay his respects, and was impressed by Stonewall's simplicity of manners and genuine courtesy. His family spent a few days with him this winter; then he first saw his infant daughter.

This was but the lull amid the storm of war, and as the season approached for the opening of the campaign, Jackson prepared to leave his pleasant winter quarters. He moved about the middle of March to Hamilton's crossing where he occupied a tent.

Hooker had now replaced Burnside in command of the Army of the Potomac, and by the end of April he was ready for the campaign with a force 132,000 strong. His army lay in camp on the left bank of the Rappahannock opposite Fredericksburg; the Confederates were intrenched on the heights across the river. This position Hooker thought was unassailable from the front, and he undertook to turn the left flank and so fall upon our rear. In the meanwhile he sent about 12,000 cavalry on an expedition to cut our communications with Richmond. On the 27th he sent the greater part of three army corps on a long detour, 27 miles above to Kelly's ford, there to cross, move down and uncover the fords below. When this was done the several commands were to move by different routes on Chancellorsville which was the place of rendezvous. This he accomplished with great skill and energy, and by the 30th he had an army of 48,000 men with 18,000 more a few hours behind, fortified at Chancellorsville in an impregnable position in the very heart of the wilderness. Hence, General Hooker from military considerations was justified in his prediction when he said: "The enemy must ingloriously fly or come out from behind his intrenchments and give us battle on our own ground, where certain destruction awaits him.''

But in his plans, perhaps, he had not made a just allowance for the genius of Stonewall Jackson.

It is a tradition that one of his officers remarked on this occasion: "We seem to have the rebs this time, and a sure victory—only I don't know where old Stonewall is—he might break in behind us here and spoil all this!"

Lee was aware that his left flank had been turned and that Hooker was in his rear with a force fully equal to his own. He ordered Early with 10,000 men to hold the heights at Fredericksburg; and with the remaining forces hastened to confront Hooker at Chancellorsville. Jackson's main force was 20 miles distant; he began to move at midnight and by 11 o'clock next day, May 1, he was drawn up in line of battle in front of the Wilderness.

Hooker, who had begun to move out into the open ground where he could handle his troops, now fell back behind his fortification of logs at Chancellorsville. He said the ways were narrow and he could not debouch from the woods rapidly enough to confront Lee, but would run the risk of being whipped in detail while filing from the narrow wood-roads.

That night Lee and Jackson camped together in the woods; they laid themselves down to rest upon the leaves with the pine-trees for covering. Their consultation was long, and anxiously did they discuss the critical situation of the armies. They both agreed that it was necessary to attack Hooker at once or all would be lost. They also agreed that an attack made in front on his stronghold would be very destructive to their troops, and would probably fail. A cavalry reconnoisance had disclosed the exposed situation of the Union right, and now they resolved to attack there.

To do this the Confederate force must be divided. Jackson with 30,000 men was to move by a forest road, known to him, entirely around the Union position and attack in the rear.

Lee, while Jackson was making his flank movement, was to keep up a show in front with only 20,000 men; it was a hazardous venture, warranted only by the desperate nature of the situation.

Jackson moved at daybreak—on this, the last day, he was to lead troops in battle—he made a circuit of 15 miles, sheltered from view by the thick undergrowth, except at one point where the road bore southward, and where his movement, if noticed, would be taken as a retreat.

By three o'clock in the afternoon he was six miles west of Chancellorsville, and on the opposite side of Hooker from the position held by Lee. He halted here in an open space to form his lines; while his scouts pushing forward through the thickets discovered the Union intrenchments unguarded; the arms were stacked, the men preparing their evening meal.

Jackson formed his force in three parallel lines with their centers resting on the narrow wood-road, down which two batteries were to move. About five o'clock the advance was begun; the line in front breaking its way through the thicket, the others following with a little less difficulty.

An hour later they burst upon the Union ranks like an avalanche—all was wild confusion! The first regiments on whom the shock fell scattered without firing a shot, while the whole corps soon broke in disorder, leaving everything behind them, swarming down the road to within a half mile of Chancellorsville. The Confederates were stayed for a brief space by the horse-artillery of Pleasanton's cavalry reinforced by other guns, but this battery in turn was hurled back; and the onset was only delayed by the darkness and confusion—awaiting a reconnoissance.

At this critical moment Jackson rode to the front to learn the situation of affairs, and on returning to his lines he was fired on by his own men who mistook his escort for enemies. He received three wounds which proved fatal a week later. Several of his escorts were killed or wounded by the same volley. As he was being carried from the field one of the litter bearers fell, and Jackson was thrown to the ground, falling upon his wounded shoulder; this aggravated his injuries and together with the loss of blood he had sustained, he was now almost in a dying condition.

General Hooker was also wounded on this day, but retained his command.

Jackson was succeeded by General J. E. B. Stuart, of the cavalry, and he had orders from Lee to press the advantages gained; this was done on all sides with this result;—at the end of three days more, Hooker's whole command of superior numbers had retired to the north side of the Rappahannock, and the battle of Chancellorsville had ended.

As soon as possible, the wounded Jackson was conveyed in an ambulance to Guinea's Station; this was a painful journey for a suffering man. The surgeons did everything to relieve him, but in vain. His wife, with infant daughter, was summoned to his bedside. He remained cheerful and was informed of the final success of his flank movement at Chancellorsville. He died as he had lived, a Christian without fear of death. His last words were: "Let us cross over the river, and rest under the shade of the trees."

Above we have given a concise presentation of the principal movements of Jackson in the course of his brilliant career; we shall now conclude these personal recollections, with a few anecdotes to illustrate further his characteristics.

*   *   *   *   *

As the war progressed and his fame grew apace, whenever he would appear riding along the lines of infantry, on his chestnut-sorrel horse, clad in his old, faded uniform, the loud cheers of his soldiers would follow him for miles along the dusty roads.

He was a good rider, but not a very graceful one except on the occasions mentioned, when the soldiers were cheering; then he would straighten himself in his saddle and ride erect with uncovered head and at a rapid pace, as if to escape this ovation of his troops.

On one occasion in the "Valley campaign," as our troops debouched from a narrow cross-road into the turnpike, we saw a carriage drawn up by the wayside, in which were seated an elderly gentleman and three young ladies. As we rode by the old gentleman halted us and inquired anxiously for General Jackson. It at first occurred to us that he had news of importance to communicate to the general, but the young ladies soon made it apparent that their only object in being in that dangerous place was to look upon this now famous officer whom they had never seen. They paid but little heed to any other officer or soldier of the passing column.

The old man "only wanted to see Jackson once before he died," and the young ladies were "just crazy to see him!"

Soon thereafter a post quartermaster rode by; his bright uniform presented a striking contrast to the dust begrimed regimentals of the officers of the column, and the young ladies "were sure this fine-looking officer must be the great 'Stonewall,'" the hero of their imaginations.

Finally, when General Jackson did appear on the scene, it was difficult to make these ladies believe that the travel stained horseman, with his faded cap drawn low over his sunburned, bearded face, was the famous "Stonewall" whose name had wrought so great a spell in that valley.

And the prestige of his fame must linger there forever; for however much one may insist that he committed a great political error in yielding paramount allegiance to his State, yet none at this day will doubt that he did so conscientiously and religiously believing that he was absolutely right. Therefore, as a great soldier performing deeds of valor with consummate skill in the line of his duty as he saw it, he will remain to military men the world over, and in American history, a figure of perennial interest.   *   *
*   *   *   From that day when at the battle of Bull Run General Bee pointed his sword and said: "See, there is Jackson standing like a stone-wall," and from which saying he won his

sobriquet, Jackson was ever wont to give the glory of victory to the Lord, and to deprecate any applauding of victorious generals. Mrs. Jackson in her "Life" says: "General D. H. Hill relates that in the last conversation he ever held with him, Jackson said: 'The manner in which the press, the army, and the people seem to lean on certain persons is positively frightful. They are forgetting God in the instruments He has chosen. It fills me with alarm.'"

Jackson was a consistent Christian man, he was a constant attendant on preaching and as a matter of duty he taught a class of negro children in the Sunday School at Lexington.

He systematically gave to the extent of his limited means, to every benevolent object. In illustration of this trait of his character, it is related that when the news reached Lexington of the victory of Manassas, it was reported that the Rev. Dr. White had received a letter from Jackson, and the people gathered around to hear the particulars of the battle.

The venerable preacher mounted on a store-box, arranged his spectacles, broke the seal of his letter and read as follows:

" MY DEAR PASTOR:
        "In my tent last night, after a fatiguing day's service, I remembered that I failed to send you my contribution for our colored Sunday School. Enclosed you will find my check for that object, which please acknowledge at your earliest convenience and oblige yours faithfully,
                        "T. J. JACKSON."

And that was all! The people were much
amused, and the old minister disconcerted by
this special communication from the battle-field.

*　　　*　　　*　　　*　　　*

It was claimed by some that Jackson was seen
in battle, and elsewhere, very frequently in the
act of prayer with his hand upraised. But this
is a mistake for he made no display of his relig-
ion. He was wounded in his hand at the first
battle of Manassas, and which, by the way, he
would not have dressed until some private soldiers more in need had been attended to, first.
This wound in his hand at times gave him pain
which was relieved somewhat by holding it upright, and thus was started the rumor, that "he
was often seen holding up his hand in prayer."
*　*　* On the day of Malvern Hill I saw
"Stonewall" Jackson in the thick of the fight and
under circumstances that stirred the depths of
his nature. The sun was sinking towards the
western sky when our wearied troops emerged
from the pine woods, which were being torn and
riven by shot and shell.

We stood there then, obscured from our formidable adversary only by the black cloud of
sulphurous smoke that overhung the bloody field
like a pall shrouding the windrows of the slain.
McClellan's grand army, 90,000 strong, con-
fronted us on those heights, which bristled with
300 field pieces and great siege guns re-inforced

by the monster cannon of the river boats. All
the guns banked in tiers, extending the distance
of a mile, now belched forth in streams of flame
and iron hail, that mowed down ranks and regiments and forest trees far in their rear. The
incessant din and concussion of the bursting
bombs seemed to rend the firmament and shake
the solid earth.

As we moved forward into action, we passed
within a few paces of "Stonewall" who, at that
time, was giving orders to a battery which was
being actually destroyed by the concentrated fire
of McClellan's artillery. He sat erect on his
horse in this hurricane of "cannister" and
"grape;" his face was aflame with passion, his
eyes flashed, his under jaw protruded, and his
voice rang out sharp and clear.

Before he was entirely obscured from our
view, the soldiers of the column would turn, at
brief intervals, to look back on him as if for the
last time; and, indeed, it was the last time for
many of us.

*   *   *   *   *

As regards Jackson's relations to General Lee
and other generals of high rank, and speaking
from the standpoint of a subordinate, it appeared
to us as if they were all more like brothers than
like rival generals.

Jackson said: "I will follow General Lee
blindfolded;" and Lee said of Jackson, after his

death: "I have lost my right arm!"—and well he might say that.　　*　　*　　*

Toward the close of his career whenever "Stonewall" Jackson appeared to citizens who had known him only by reputation, he was always regarded by them with great interest. Many had clothed him in imagination with almost supernatural powers; others believed him to be a chosen leader, especially favored of heaven on account of his religious character and pure life.

But his soldiers knew that his success lay in his eternal vigilance, his untiring energy, his personal supervision and perfect knowledge of the topography of the field of his operations, and in the exercise of those qualities that bring success to other generals. Yet he possessed qualities that were peculiar to him as natural gifts; he had a resolute mind and never halted between two opinions; and he had the intuitions and instincts of the born soldier, quick to discover, and to take advantage of any mistakes his adversary might make　Above all, he had a realizing sense of the inestimable value of time in connection with the operations of war. He was always on time. It was a tradition with his soldiers that when at Richmond Lee heard the sound of Jackson's guns, away off on McClellan's right, he took out his watch and calmly remarked: "Jackson is on time."

General Lee knew all that this remark implied

—the arduous toil and sleepless energy—yet he expressed no surprise; he expected nothing less of Jackson. * * * * *

It is related that Jackson on his tour of Europe visited the battle-field of Waterloo. He was familiar with the details of that battle, as he was of others, for although a devout, humble Christian, he was essentially a military man and took delight in military affairs, and was a student of the campaigns of history. He pointed out at Waterloo, how Napoleon had tarried too long at Hougoumont, and how the delay to begin the battle early in the morning—rain or no rain —proved fatal; and other sagacious remarks that showed him to be conversant with the situation. But he believed that the brilliant Napoleon, through failing health, was not himself on that field, and that he did not there display the military acumen and the towering genius that had glorified other fields.

And it may be said that in some characteristics, these two great military geniuses were not unlike; Jackson's confidence in himself, under Supreme guidance, in all his military maneuvres was not unlike Napoleon's faith in his star of destiny; yet it may be remarked that neither of them, despite all this, ever failed in any precaution that might tend to his success in battle.

They each believed in officers who could

accomplish things; that achievement was worth all, and unfulfilled promises, nothing.

Napoleon thought a blunder in military affairs worse than a deliberate crime; Jackson would make no allowance for an officer who failed in an enterprise through any neglect of duty, however arduous the duty might be, if it could be accomplished at all, through strenuous and persevering exertion.

He never spared himself any trouble or exertion, and was often thoroughly worn out by incessant labors, and by hunger and loss of sleep; as the following anecdote will go to show:

Shortly after sunrise, on the morning after the battle of Fredericksburg, as I was walking along the ridge above Hamilton's Crossing, and about thirty yards from one of our batteries, I passed within a few feet of General Jackson who had taken up his position on this vantage ground for the purpose of reconnoitering; but he was not doing very much of it just at that time, for he was seated on the ground, leaning against a hickory sapling, and fast asleep! He held his bridle-rein in one hand and his field-glass in the other, and did not awaken as I walked along the path in touching distance of him, but seemed to be sleeping as calmly as I had seen him sleep years before in the church at Lexington.

However, his slumbers were destined to be of short duration, for a battery of heavy guns on the Stafford heights soon opened with a volley directed against the battery near the spot where Jackson was quietly sleeping. The fire of these guns continued only for a short time, but while it lasted the din was terrific, not to speak of the destruction wrought by the hurtling missiles. The very first gun that opened this morning salute sent a shell right into the muzzle of the cannon nearest the general, broke it from its trunnions, and hurled the piece back into the barbette, killing two horses, and barely missing the cannoneers who were trenching at the time, an operation they could not perform the day before while the battle was raging.

Several days after this I met General Jackson riding across the battle field about two miles below Fredericksburg. He was riding alone and very slowly, with his head hanging down as if in profound thought. He halted a few minutes and spoke in a friendly, kindly way, but made no allusion to the battle, the sad, melancholy evidences of which were all around us.   *   *   *   *   *

A few weeks before his death I visited his head-quarters for the last time. He at that time occupied for his office, an out building at Moss Neck on the Rappahannock, which had been used in happier days as a sporting lodge. On the walls of this room still hung pictures of race horses, game cocks and the trophies of the chase.

One was impressed on entering here with the ludicrous incongruity of these pictures to the grim surroundings of war, and to the taste of the grave, religious soldier who occupied these quarters. After a pleasant conversation of half an hour I took my leave of General Jackson, who had now won a world wide fame, and was still the same modest diffident man I had met for the first time at Lexington, eleven years before.   *   *   *   *   *

When Jackson died many of his friends believed that his death portended the downfall of his cause, and never had much hope of its success from that fatal day; but his soldiers grieved his loss as no others could grieve for him. His death smote the whole south-land "with a pang of unspeakable anguish."

He died at Guinea's Station, near Fredericksburg, May 10, 1863.   *   *   *   *

The Duke of Wellington once expressed the opinion that the presence of Napoleon on a field of battle was worth all of 20,000 men. It would be difficult to compute how many men the presence of Jackson on a battlefield was worth. There was but one "Stonewall" Jackson. His presence in any battle where the victory wavered in the balance, his soldiers thought, was worth all the difference between victory and defeat.

"Brave men lived before Agamemnon," and there were brave and able officers living after

Jackson, but his constant success had wrought such faith in his old soldiers, and they were so dazzled by the popular applause and enthusiasm which his presence everywhere inspired that they truly believed there was none to come after him that could fill his place.

NOTE. A portion of this narrative (illustrated,) is published in the war-book entitled, "Under Both Flags."

SONNET.

"STONEWALL" JACKSON.

Jackson stands there, "like a stone wall," he said,
As he pointed his sword across the battlefield;
Thus the name—none prouder on spotless shield
Than "Stonewall," the sobriquet to valor paid.
Twas ever thus where heroes have drawn the blade;
The gentle were the daring when dangers appealed,
And Jackson, the devout, the lion-heart revealed,
As he stood at Manassas with his old brigade!
He wrote with the sword in rude columns of war,
And the trace he made may grow dim on the scroll
Of time, as the generations rise and fall;
Yet the memories of heroic deeds reach afar,
And with the noble and the true on honor's roll,
"Stonewall" will abide till the last call.

SKETCHES

OF

TRAVEL AND BIOGRAPHY,

PART II.

PART II.

ACROSS THE OCEAN.

We took passage at New York on a Cunarder, and as the pilot stood at the helm and steered the ship through the countless craft that thronged the bay, many friends upon the dock waved adieu to friends on board, and my companion must need wave too, although we had no friend there to bid us good-bye. We steamed down the bay past the busy wharfs, in sight of the Brooklyn bridge, past the Statue of Liberty, Staten Island and through the Narrows with its forts and bristling guns, and so on through the lower bay. When we had crossed the bar and were well off Sandy Hook, and just as our harbor pilot had left us, to our surprise our ship hove to and cast anchor. We were informed that we were to await in the offing the through mail from Australia via. California, which was several hours late.

Thus the first night on the ship we slept upon the bosom of comparatively smooth waters, but when we awoke the mail had been taken aboard, and our vessel was ploughing the waves under a full head of steam. Although the sailors said it was smooth sailing, the waters seemed rough to us, and before the day was over many passengers were very sea-sick; and some thought in their extremity if their feet were firm set on the land, they would not again venture upon the treacherous waves.

After a day or two the majority of the passengers came around again all right, and to those who were not effected by mal-de-mer, the sea-air was very stimulating and seemed to whet the appetite to an unusual degree.

There were a large number of passengers representing many nationalities, yet there was no jar or discord among them for it seemed to be the rule for each one to do what he could to contribute to the enjoyment of all, and many hours were whiled away in reading, singing, pitching rings, shuffle-board, and at playing the American game of draw poker in the smoking room where many sovereigns changed hands.

An incident of some interest occurred when we were about one hundred miles out from New York harbor—a carrier pigeon was turned loose at that point. It was the intention of the owner that it should bear a message to a town in the interior of New Jersey. The bird arose high in the air, and then after circling around for a time it seemed to take its bearings and bore away backward on the course whence we came. Long afterwards we learned from the owner that the bird did actually make the Jersey coast, but there unfortunately it was discovered by a boy hunter as it rested after its long stormy flight and was shot. The hunter, however, he said, had the grace to send the message it carried (wrapped around its legs) to his family in the interior.

Our captain, a bluff English mariner about forty-five years of age, read the Episcopal service on Sunday in the dining saloon. He read it with gravity and impressively, yet it smacked somewhat of the flavor of the sea. An elderly English clergyman preached the sermon; the day was stormy and the rolling ship pitched the Bible from the improvised altar. The aged minister dropped his "h's" badly in speech, yet he proved to be a man of classical culture, and before the close he spoke with impassioned eloquence.

In passing the Grand Banks the fog was thick and the ship's bell was sounded every few minutes. We saw here a number of fishing smacks and one small boat containing two men floated very near our ship.

The bronzed fishermen saluted the passing vessel by doffing their hats, and one of them held up to view a very large fish. This incident called to mind the fact, that upon a late voyage one of the vessels of this line picked up two fishermen who had drifted for three days lost in the fog, and were nearly famished. They were treated kindly, as is the custon on the sea; the passengers raised a handsome collection for them, and they and their boat were taken to Liverpool and placed in the great "Exposition of Navigation," which at that time was being held there. They were certainly genuine specimens of Newfoundland fishermen and fishing boat.

Although we crossed the ocean afterwards, yet first impressions are the best, at least the most vivid; and never again did we see so much life on the sea as on this first voyage. Our vessel had sailed a more northern route than usual to avoid the icebergs that were known to be in the track usually taken. In this northern route, porpoises played around our ship daily, also stormy petrel and sea gulls skimmed the waves near by, and sharks, large "man-eaters," would occasionally dart past the ship with incredible velocity. But the greatest sight of all was reserved for a certain beautiful afternoon when we were all seated on the promenade deck; a large whale rose in full view not fifty yards away; it rested quite still for a short time, and as the passengers rushed to the guards it fell astern, spouting vigorously. We all had a fine view of it.

It was nearly nightfall when we sighted the

heights of Cape Clear Island, the outermost point of Ireland—"Green Erin," whose many woes since the days of Cromwell have excited the sympathies of the world. Her cause has never lacked champions, martyrs and silver-tongued orators, such as Emmet, Burke, Curran and Sheridan, and in our time Parnell and Gladstone.

The darkness had about shrouded the scene as we came under "Fastnet Light," which is on a rock twelve miles off the coast and sixty miles from Queenstown. The lighthouse stands high above the water on a rock barely large enough to hold it, and is in appearance lonely and picturesque.

The mails are put off at Queenstown, which is a strongly fortified, landlocked harbor, 253 miles from Liverpool. They are carried thence by train to Kingston, across the Irish Sea to Holy Head, thence to London by train, arriving there twenty-four hours before the passengers who go up the channel.

All day Sunday we steamed up St. George's Channel and the Irish Sea, arriving at the Liverpool docks about five p. m. This is in some respects the greatest sea-port of the world; the cut stone docks extend a distance of twelve miles, and more craft resort to this harbor than to any other.

We arrived in London about ten a. m. the next day. This city is a world within itself, con-

taining now 5,657,000 people; twenty-eight miles
of street are built each year, on an average, and
it is said that its beer shops if placed side by
side would extend a distance of seventy-five
miles. For antiquities and historical associations, this city surpasses in interest any other
English speaking city of the earth.

In walking these streets we passed Whitehall,
in front of which Charles I was executed, and
here also a few years later, the head of Cromwell was displayed on a pike in the old Whitehall Chamber. We can scarcely realize at this
day that such things could be. We noticed the
sign of "Dombey & Son," and thought of Mr.
Dickens; we walked by "Old Curiosity Shop,"
and thought of "Little Nell;" this latter building is low, dingy, and insignificant in appearance.

In the early morning we walked across Westminster Bridge which Wordsworth has commem-
orated in the lines of a beautiful poem; also, we
crossed the ancient London Bridge, and entered
the celebrated Billingsgate fish-market, but it
was rather late, and business of the day was well
over. Next we ascended the ancient "London
Monument," near the Tower, which marks the
spot where the great fire, that destroyed so
large a portion of the city in 1666, was stopped.

The London streets indeed abound in traditions and vestiges of antiquity. We were

standing on the steps of St. Paul's after having viewed the graves of Nelson and Wellington, the battle-scarred flags of the Crimean War, and other relics of that ancient church, when there passed us a little group of countrymen led by a guide. We turned and followed into the church; they passed everything without notice, until, on turning aside into the transcept, the guide halted in front of the tomb of the Duke of Wellington.

He said: "Here is the man who whipped Bonaparte!" The majority of these vistors were evidently unable to read, but they crowded with great interest about the tomb of Wellington. They talked boastfully of the man "who had whipped old Bony;" then, after spending all of a half hour around this grave, they left the church without looking at anything else.

We took this opportunity to copy into our note-book the epitaph on the monument recently erected here, to "Chinese" Gordon. There is, perhaps, nowhere to be found a more truthful, or a nobler epitaph than this to General Gordon. It is as follows:

GENERAL CHARLES GEORGE GORDON,
of Soudan fame, by his brother.

He gave his strength to the weak; his service to the poor; his sympathy to the suffering; his heart to God. At last obedient to the commands of his sovereign, he died to save women and children from imminent death and suffering.

TOWER OF LONDON.

The Tower of London is the most ancient palace and fortress in England; its origin is ascribed to Julius Cæsar. Other writers claim that the White Tower is the oldest part, and that it was built by William the Conqueror in 1078.

Macaulay in his History of England, says of the burials in the ancient chapel: "Thither have been carried through successive ages by the rude hands of gaolers, without one mourner following, the bleeding relics of men who have been the captains of armies, the leaders of parties, the oracles of senates and the ornaments of courts;" and again he says: "In truth there is no sadder spot on earth than this little cemetery."

In the midst of the "Tower green" is planted a brass tablet on which we read this inscription:

"SITE OF ANCIENT SCAFFOLD
ON THIS SPOT
QUEEN ANNE BOLEYN
WAS BEHEADED ON THE
19TH OF MAY 1536"

This is the style and form of the inscription, without one punctuation mark. It tells a sad truth, but not the whole truth, for Queen Katharine, Lady Jane Grey and others were also executed on this spot.

The dark and winding passageways of the Tower are now lighted by electricity. In our rambles here we took note of many relics of a barbarous age, the horrid implements of torture used in the olden time; the "scavenger's daughter," a rough iron implement for securing the neck, arms and feet of the victim; the "bilboes" used for fastening prisoners together; the "thumb screws," and the "collar of torment."

The crown jewels or the regalia are kept here in the Wakefield Tower. The crown, scepter and various regalia worn at coronations are here to be seen; but most of the magnificent objects date from the time of the restoration. For it is recorded that, "on the return of Charles II there existed only some loose stones and some fragments of the ancient crowns previously preserved in the Tower."

One of the most prominent objects is the crown of Queen Victoria which she used at her coronation in 1838. Many of the jewels it contains are of great antiquity. Many brilliants surround the ancient and famous ruby that once belonged to the "Black Prince," and was also worn in the helmet of Henry V at the battle of Agincourt.

Victoria's crown is said to contain precious

stones as follows: diamonds 2783; pearls 277; rubies 5; sapphires 17; emeralds 11. It presents an appearance, though tasteful, gorgeous in the extreme.

It would take long to merely glance at the numerous crowns, scepters, communion service, swords, bracelets, spurs of gold, &c., &c., that are preserved in the iron cage of this great stronghold, surrounded by guards. We shall note only one or two more.

The "Annointing Spoon" is said to be one of the few objects remaining of the old regalia of remote times. It is of solid gold, the bowl is beautifully chased, and the handle enameled and set with jewels.

The salt-cellar of gold, richly jewelled, was modelled after the White Tower. It was used at state banquets and served to mark the seats of honor, "above the salt."

In the armory in the White Tower among the innumerable knights and figures in armor, there is an effigy of Queen Elizabeth mounted upon her palfrey, as she appeared in going to Westminster Abbey to return thanks for the repulse of the Spanish Armada in 1588.

It is surprising how small the suits of armor are; scarcely any of them are large enough to fit a man of medium stature of this age. We noticed also that the soldiers on guard at the outer tower would have to stoop their shoulders as they entered beneath the archway of the ancient guard-room. The modern man is evidently of greater stature than the men for whom this guard-room was built many centuries ago.

However, we noticed critically a splendid suit of armor of Henry VIII presented to him by Maximilian on his marriage to Katharine of Arragon. If this armor was made for him, he must have been a man of goodly size, at least six feet in height.

An Arabic coat of arms bore this curious inscription engraved on a plate attached to the chain mail:

> "Honor is obedience (to God)
> and wealth is contentment—
> health and welfare."

Here is the beheading-block, the ax and the mask worn by the executioner at the last execution of this character in Great Britain. On this block were beheaded the Scotch lords, Kilmarnock and Balmerino, adherents of Prince Charles Edward, after the battle of Culloden in the year 1746. The following year the old Scotch lord, Lovat, was beheaded on the same block. We counted six deep indentations on the block which were made by the headsman's ax; hence the average was two strokes each.

Walpole relates several eccentric traits of these Scotch lords on their trial and execution. It seems that it was the custom to carry the heads-

man's ax into the court room with the prisoners on each day of their trial; for he says:
"When they were brought from the Tower in
separate coaches, there was some dispute in
which the ax must go—old Balmerino cried,
'Come, come, put it with me.' At the bar he
played with his fingers on the ax while he talked
to the jailer. One day somebody coming up to
listen, he took the blade and held it like a fan
between their faces. At the trial in Westminster,
one day a little boy stood near him, but was not
tall enough to see; he made room for the child
and placed him near himself. He said that one
of his reasons for his pleading 'not guilty' was,
that 'so many ladies might not be disappointed
of their show.'"

Balmerino kept up his spirits to the same
pitch of gayety. In the cell at Westminster,
while waiting on the court for sentence after
their conviction, he showed Lord Kilmarnock how
he must lay his head; bid him not to wince lest
the stroke should cut his skull or his shoulders,
and advised him to bite his lips. After sentence,
as they were about to return to the Tower, he
begged they might have another bottle together,
as they should never meet anymore till—then
pointed to his neck. On arriving at the Tower,
he said to the jailer as he got out of the coach,
"Take care, or you'll break my shins with this
d—d ax." When they brought in his death-war-

rant to read to him, he was seated at dinner. His wife fainted. He jumped up to her assistance, and said: "Lieutenant, with your d—d warrant you have spoilt my lady's stomach."

On the day of their execution, as he took leave of Lord Kilmarnock for the last time, he said: "My Lord, I wish I could suffer for both!" He died with the intrepidity of a hero.

Lord Lovat was executed on Tower Hill on the same block, and with the same ax here to be seen, in April of the next year, 1747. This was the last use of the beheading-block in England; and while standing here in the Tower, viewing the ax and the block, we were forcibly reminded of the incidents here narrated.

In the state prison room the name "IANE," in ancient characters, is cut in the wall; it attracts much attention from visitors, for it is supposed that this name was cut here by Lord Guildford Dudley, when he was confined in a separate prison from his unhappy wife. This is the only memorial preserved of Lady Jane Grey in the Tower.

Queen Anne Boleyn was kept a prisoner in the royal apartments of the Tower before and after she was condemned to death; she was beheaded, as stated, "on the Green by the White Tower," less than four years after her marriage to Henry VIII.

Ancient accounts describe Queen Anne as very

beautiful; one writer speaks of her as "rivalling Venus." But a lady of the time writes, in reference to Mistress Anne's flirtations with King Henry VIII, in her diary: "Mistress Ann is not his spouse yet, nor ever will be, I hope."

But Mistress Anne drew the king deeper by her wiles, until he was forced to such declarations as follows: "My heart and I surrender themselves into your hands, and we supplicate to be commended to your good graces, and that by absence your affection may not be diminished to us, for that would be to augment our pain, which would be a great pity, since absence gives enough, and more than I ever thought could be felt, &c."

An ancient account says in regard to her execution, that proper preparations had not been made and that "her body was thrown into an elm chest to put arrows in, and was buried in the Chapel of the Tower before twelve o'clock."

Of all the distinguished men that were confined in the Tower, perhaps Sir Walter Raleigh is the most interesting character. He was imprisoned for twelve years in the Bloody Tower. It was here he was visited by Prince Henry, who one day said to an attendant as he left the presence of Sir Walter: "No king, save my father, would keep such a bird in such a cage." Sir Walter devoted much of his time to chemistry, and the Lieutenant of the Tower wrote of him: "He has converted a little hen-house in the garden into a still-house, and here he doth spend his time all the day in distillations. * * * * he doth show himself upon the wall in his garden to the view of the people." Here he wrote political discourses and commenced his "History."

On the morning of his execution, it is related that his keeper brought him a cup of sack, and inquired how he liked it; he said, "it was a good drink, if a man might tarry by it." As he trod the scaffold, he touched the ax and said: "This is sharp medicine, but it will cure all diseases."

The Bishop of Salisbury who attended at his execution, declared: "His was the most fearless of deaths that ever was known and the most resolute and confident, yet with reverence and conscience!"

Many visitors read in the Beauchamp Tower, the pathetic inscriptions that were carved on these walls by prisoners who were never more to breathe the free air. The descendants of the men who persecuted them, pay a small sum to come here now and read these tangible evidences of their despair.

The one thought that impresses the student of humanity, while walking through the gloomy passages of these ancient prisons and palaces is, that the world is certainly better now than it used to be; at least, it is more refined in its cruelties.

WESTMINSTER ABBEY.

To an American traveler who is concerned in the past history of his race, there is no more interesting spot on earth than Westminster Abbey; for he will perceive here–exemplified by tangible objects the continuity of England's history during a period of a thousand years.

Throughout these centuries the chief actors in great historic events—their careers ended—have been brought here for interment. Not only the mortal remains of kings and queens but of soldiers, scholars and poets: men of action and men of thought; the greatest of their time, rest here.

Here then, the intelligent American traveler will be stirred by the memories of the past as nowhere else on his journey; and to this spot he will turn with the deepest interest.

This venerable and splendid edifice was originally founded by Segbert, King of the East Saxons. It was rebuilt by Edward the Confessor; after his time it was destroyed by fire, and again rebuilt during the reign of the three Edwards. In the reign of Henry VII, that monarch added the chapel known by his name, and it finally came under the care of the great architect, Sir Christopher Wren.

The architectural order is Gothic, and its walls are built of cream-colored sandstone called "Caen Stone."

The best view of the Abbey externally is from the open space in front of the western entrance. Entering here, the body of the church presents a grand and impressive appearance; the whole design being at once opened to the view; its lofty roof, beautifully colored lights, and long arcades of columns.

The present church is not the work of one generation, but of five centuries. In the year 1478 Edward IV wrote to the Pope at Rome, in which letter he speaks of the Abbey as "placed before the eyes of the whole world of Englishmen," and to which any favor shown would be "welcome to all of English blood."

Thus we see, the interest now so widely felt in this venerable church has existed throughout generations. During these years the great victories won by English armies have been celebrated by processions and Te Deums beneath its roof.

The Chapter House of the Abbey where Parliament frequently assembled for three centuries, may well be called "the cradle of Parliamentary government" of England and her Colonies. Also through many centuries this stately edifice has been the scene of coronations, royal marriages, and funerals.

The principal points of interest are The Nave, Henry VII Chapel, Confessor's Chapel, Poet's Corner and Jerusalem Chamber.

Henry VII erected this Chapel as a place of burial for himself and sovereigns of England. It is even yet—though frayed and dimmed by time—one of the most exquisite specimens of florid Gothic architecture. Its walls are covered with a lace-like pattern, and every part is enriched with a minute tracery and hundreds of roses, portcullises, fleur-de-lis and grey-hounds; emblems of the royal families represented.

The windows are filled with painted glass, and the light which streams through them is tinged with a glow of warm colors that heighten the effect of the scene.

Henry VII was buried here on the 10th of May, 1509, in a gorgeous shrine inlaid with gold and silver. But the rude soldiery of the Civil War stripped off the gold and silver wherever they could find it, and they marred and obliterated much of the beauty of this tomb, as well as of others which have been fashioned by hands of unequalled skill.

Cromwell's Roundheads showed but scanty respect for monuments and memorials.

As side by side they recline upon their tomb, the effigies of King Henry VII and his queen, even to this day excite the deepest admiration. It is said that muscular modelling and anatomy were sculptured here for the first time, true to nature. Bacon speaks of this tomb as "one of the stateliest and daintiest monuments of Europe."

Henry VII entered into a formal written agreement with the Monastery of Westminster, as to the religious observances to be held in this chapel "whilst the world shall endure," notwithstanding this, in less than fifty years after his death, "the last flicker of the tapers had died out at his shrine."

Near by in the white marble tomb erected by James I rest the bodies of Queen Elizabeth and her half-sister, Queen Mary, in the same grave. On this tomb reclines the magnificent effigy of the haughty Queen Elizabeth, carved in Parian marble.

This tomb bears the following Latin inscription: "*Regno consortes et urna, hic abdorimus Elizabetha et Maria sorores, in spe reserrectionis.*"

Dean Stanley remarked on this pathetic epitaph: "The long war of the English Reformation isc losed in these words. The sisters are at one, the daughter of Katharine of Arragon and the daughter of Anne Boleyn rest in peace, at last."

It is a singular fact that the last royal tombs erected in the Abbey, are the one of Elizabeth and

Mary, and the one adjoining which contains the remains of Mary Queen of Scotts. On this tomb which was also erected by James I in honor of his mother, rests the exquisite marble effigy of that beautiful, unfortunate queen.

Fourteen sovereigns have sat on the throne since Elizabeth, yet no monument has been erected here to any one of them, not so much as even a line of inscription carved!

At coronations that have taken place since the time of Edward I in Westminster, the monarch has always been seated in a large oaken chair, called "King Edward's chair."

This chair is very quaintly carved and is now dark with age. It was made for Edward I as a coronation chair and contains an under seat on which rests the "Scone stone," which is in appearance a limestone. Its history is briefly as follows: When Edward I overran Scotland in the year 1297, he seized this precious stone on which the Scotch monarchs had been crowned for many generations, and took it to England where it was placed in Westminster Abbey.

The funeral of Henry V was the most imposing, perhaps, ever held in Westminster up to that time. His three chargers were led up to the altar behind his effigy, which was dressed in royal robes and lay on the splendid car; "accompained by white robed priests innumerable."

Five hundred men-at-arms dressed in black,

with lances reversed, and three hundred more with torches, made an impressive scene. The funeral helmet, saddle and shield of this warrior king were hung on a cross-beam, where although frayed and falling to pieces from age, they are still to be seen in their places. Dean Stanley refers to this helmet as, "the very casque that did affright the air at Agincourt!"

Literary associations are connected in our minds with Westminster Abbey almost as closely as the historical memorials which crowd its walls. The American visitor here for the first time anticipates joyously the prospect of looking on the famous "Poets' Corner."

And the very first tomb he will come to is that of Geoffrey Chaucer, the father of English poetry. He died in 1400 and his was the first tomb in Poets' Corner. Two hundred years later, Edmund Spenser, the next great poet after Chaucer, was buried here near his tomb. An ancient poet wrote in Latin verse: "He was the nearest to Chaucer in genius and it is meet that his grave should be next to his." Drayton said of him: "Master Edmund Spenser has done enough for the immortality of his name had he only given us his Shepherd's Calendar."

It is a tradition that Drayton, together with his companions, Ben Jonson and Shakespeare, attended the funeral of Spenser. For an ancient account says: "Poets attended upon his hearse, and mournful elegies with the pens that wrote them, were thrown into his tomb!"

If it were so that records are as imperishable in the dust of Westminster as in the sands of Egypt—then this tomb of the poet Spenser should be unclosed to recover the "mournful elegy" written by the hand of Shakespeare!

Clustered near by the tombs of Chaucer and Spenser are the monuments or cenotaphs of Shakespeare, Milton, Ben Jonson, Campbell, etc., down to our own time: such as Tennyson, Macaulay, Beaconsfield, Dickens, Browning and our own Longfellow and Lowell. Very few of them are buried here.

Ben Jonson, the friend of Shakespeare, was buried here in the "Nave," Poets' Corner, in an upright position and a modern paving stone now marks the place. The ancient stone that covered his remains was placed in its present position against the wall in 1821 to preserve its incription: "O rare Ben Jonson!"

His singular burial in a standing position is explained as follows: One day being rallied by the Dean of Westminster about being buried in "Poets' Corner," the poet is said to have replied: "I am too poor for that and no one will lay out funeral charges upon me. No sir, six feet long by two feet wide is too much for me; two feet by two will do for all I want."

"You shall have it," said the Dean, and thus the conversation ended.

The world famous inscription: "O rare Ben Jonson," has been attributed to Sir William Davenant, who succeeded Jonson as poet laureate and on whose tomb is found the same expression, "O rare Sir William Davenant!"

Shakespeare's monument, erected more than a hundred years after his death, was called by Horace Walpole, "a preposterous monument," —this phrase may be applicable to it. However, there is a compensation in the circumstance that on the scroll held by his life-size effigy, there are engraved his own immortal lines—peculiarly applicable to these surroundings where earthly grandeur is fading away.

"The cloud-capped towers, the gorgeous palaces,
The solemn temples, the great globe itself,
Yea; all which it inherit shall dissolve,
And, like this insubstantial pageant faded,
Leave not a rack behind."

The tomb of Edward I, the greatest of the Plantagenets, is the plainest of all the royal tombs,—a simple box-like coffin of stone; but it bears the following epitaph, which is said to be the most stirring of those which belong to the Reformation period: "*Edvardus Primus, malleus Scotorum, hic est Pactum serva.*"

The lines on the monument of Oliver Goldsmith, written by his friend Dr. Johnson, have been thought very fine; in fact, many have searched for them in vain among the classics, as others have done for Sterne's "shorn lamb," in the Bible. They are as follows:

"*Qui nullum fere scribendi genus non tetigit, nullum tetigit quod non ornavit.*" That is to say: "Who left scarcely any style of writing untouched, and touched nothing that he did not adorn."

Another quaint epitaph, expressed so nobly by an unknown author of the seventeenth century, is inscribed on the tomb of the Duchess of Newcastle, as follows: "She was a wise and learned lady, as her many books do testify, and was the youngest sister of a noble family; all the brothers were valiant and all the sisters virtuous."

The bust of the American poet, Longfellow, was placed here two years after his death, "by his English admirers."

One has been recently erected to the American writer Lowell, who became popular as minister to England, also in literature. These comprise the only monuments to Americans, but there are a number here to individuals who have been connected with our history.

In the North Transept stands a lofty monument to the Earl of Chatham, the "Great Commoner," and the friend of the American colonies. His last speech was in the House of Lords in 1778, when, in a dying condition, he insisted on coming to oppose Lord North's government. After delivering his great historic appeal in defense of the American colonies, he fell down in his seat from exhaustion, and died a few weeks afterwards.

Here is a monument to Major Andre, Adjutant General of the British forces in North America. As is well known, he was captured while on a secret mission to Arnold at West Point. After a trial by court martial, he was condemned and hung as a spy. His monument was erected at the expense of George III, and forty years afterward his remains were brought here and interred near its base. On this shaft, there is a bas-relief likeness of Washington receiving the petition in which Andre implored for a soldier's rather than a felon's death. There is on the opposite side a bas-relief representing Andre on the way to execution.

On the monument of Handel, the composer, there is engraved on the stone scroll before him, the text with notes: "I know that my Redeemer liveth," which he so grandly illustrated by the music of his "Messiah."

The marble tiles of this historic edifice have been worn by the foot-steps of those who themselves, "after life's fitful fever," have found graves or cenotaphs beneath its roof. The learned Elizabeth, Shakespeare, Milton, Ben Jonson, Dryden, Scott, Macaulay, Thackeray, Tennyson, and Dickens have all walked here while reading the inscriptions on these ancient tombs.

THE BATTLEFIELD OF
WATERLOO.

We could not leave Brussels without visiting the battle field of Waterloo. Here, where in June, 1815, the united nations drew the sword against Napoleon, and 72,000 French faced the English and allies numbering 70,000 men, now grow broad fields of golden grain.

On that 18th day of June, thousands of horsemen had gathered here, and here was "the gallop, the charge, and the might of the fight."

We drove out to the battlefield with a small party of tourists; the distance from the city is fifteen miles, and the road winds through parks and the famous woods of Soignies. All agreed that it was a most picturesque and enjoyable ride, and a few men of the party who were interested in this world famous battle, were more or less excited by anticipation of the scene they were to look upon, after passing the village of Waterloo.

We stopped at this village, and inspected the house in which Wellington slept the night after the battle. He reached this place about midnight of that memorable day, and dated his despatches from "Waterloo," announcing his victory, which circumstance gave the name to the battle.

The village has not changed much perhaps, since his day, and is quaint and old-fashioned in every respect. The bed upon which he slept after his great victory is still here—an ancient common bedstead, very plain, like every thing else in this humble house—common, and of rough and ancient workmanship.

As we passed on from here the broad fields opened before us, now covered with golden grain almost ready for the harvest. Wheat, barley, oats and red clover waved to the wind where the charging squadron had trampled the blood-stained earth, on the 18th of June, 1815.

We went all over the battlefield, and tarried long at Hougoumont, where the French had tarried too long on that fateful day. We walked across the plain where Ney, "The Bravest of the Brave," had led the desperate charges, and where the "Old Guard" had "died."

We stood at the spot where Wellington had given the command to the Scotch Grenadiers, in the patois of the guide: "Oop guarrd and at 'em, and de guarrds joost joomp oop, and shoot boom, boom!"

The famous "Sunken road" does not appear to us a very formidable obstacle, as our cavalry in the late war did at times charge over rougher places than this; but the plain has been some-

what lowered to the road, by taking off earth
to make the huge Belgian mount, on which rests
the great lion.

The fanciful description of Waterloo by Victor
Hugo in his *Les Miserables* is commonly accepted as a real description of the battle.
From his account of it, one might well conclude
that he had not been on this field at all.   But
we were shown a brief autograph letter of his,
in which he states that he was well pleased with
the little hotel at the foot of the Belgian mount,
where his autograph is preserved in a frame as
a precious relic.

This mound, which was erected by the Bel-
gians and on top of which rests an immense
Belgian lion in bronze, occupies the center of
the battle-field.   From this summit one can view
the whole scene.

It is a beautiful prospect now, but on that
fateful day it was a sight to stir the soldiers'
blood; when twenty thousand cavalry spurred
across these fields—the Cuirassiers in their bur-
nished armor, the Chasseurs in blue and gold,
and the red Lancers—all the veterans of many
battles—and directed by a general before that
time invincible—and who swept obstacles from
his path as the tornado sweeps the sea!

Now, all is peace.   Hougoumont is here, and
La Belle Alliance, the sunken road, and La
Haye Sainte—but the soldiers are gone; and the

blue sky is above, and the golden grain below.

Our guide on this historic field was the son of a man who had witnessed the battle, and who had acted as a guide to Generals Grant and Sheridan when they visited Waterloo.

Only a few weeks before our visit here we had stood on the field of Gettysburg. These battle-fields are not dissimilar, only Gettysburg is more broken and less favorable to equality in battle than Waterloo.

When we are informed that as many men were slain here in one day as fell on the field of Gettysburg in three days' battle, we begin to realize the nature and extent of the terrible struggle that changed the whole map of Europe.

We saw many relics for sale here—of course they are all manufactured for the purpose—still, they "come from Waterloo" and American and English travelers will buy them.

In the "Grand Place" in Brussels, we saw the building where it is said the Duchess of Richmond held the ball the night before Waterloo, and which is preserved in Byron's magnificent description in Childe Harold.

SWITZERLAND.

We arrived in Lucerne last night, having come from Heidelburg, where we had spent a day or two pleasantly. We visited the old castle of Heidelburg, the most massive and picturesque ruin in Germany. The whole surroundings of this ancient castle, with its ruined towers, moats, bridges and background of mountains covered with forests, present a picture wild and strange.

One of the notable relics of the castle is the "Great Tun," which holds 49,000 gallons of wine.

The University of Heidelburg is the most ancient and one of the largest of this empire. We noted here as one of the curious features the "student's prison," the interior walls of which were covered over with pencil sketches, crude paintings and inscriptions in German, Latin, French and a few in English.

We could not understand very well why it was necessary to have a prison for University students; but later on we came to the conclusion that it was an appropriate and useful institution; at least this was our thought after viewing

the beer-drinking and duelling of these wild
blades.

It so happened that we visited the students'
quarters beyond the Necker just at a time when
they seemed to be having—what they would
call—a good time, as they were engaged in the serious business of drinking beer and fighting duels.

One young man—a fair-haired, manly looking
fellow—who had just finished a duel, had his
scalp padded with raw cotton, and upon his
cheek were several clean cuts of the rapier—
while the cloth upon his shoulder was saturated
with his young blood. It seemed a strange
thing to us who had seen soldiers put forth their
strength in battle—this mimicry of war.

Yet it somewhat tests the native metal of the
young combatant, and to his phlegmatic German temperament brings a glory and an honor,
almost equal to that the soldier wins in the
press of charging squadrons.

The eyes of the fencers are protected by gog-
gles, and the throat and the upper part of the
chest are padded, to secure protection against a
mortal wound.

A duel began shortly after our arrival. One
of the combatants was a left-handed young man,
and the other larger and apparently braver in
the start, but the tables were soon turned. The
thrusts of the left-handed fencer are difficult to
parry as a usual thing, and it proved so in this

instance. But really these students did not "thrust" at all, as that would inevitably result in severe or mortal wounds while fencing with sharp-pointed weapons. They simply slashed away at each other over hand, but with such quick and skillful cuts as to prove them masters of fence.

The left-handed combatant soon slashed his opponent upon the cheek with a vicious stroke of his rapier that laid it open and made the blood spurt. Then the seconds interposed between them their own crossed rapiers and stopped the fight. After the wounded swordsman had been sponged off and examined by the surgeon, the fray was continued in the same manner, with pauses between wounds, to see if they were serious—and thus the fight went on, until the worsted swordsman was bleeding from many wounds—such ugly cuts as would scar his head and face for life.

We thought the above scene was a pretty lively introduction to Heidelburg, about whose classic shades we had been reading from early youth.

At night we drove over the Necker again, to view the illumination on the opposite heights. This illumination is given annually by the citizens in honor of the students, after they have passed their examinations.

From our observation of these same students

we began to rate them as pretty lively chaps, and concluded there ought to be nothing tame in an illumination given in their honor—and there was not.

At the signal, the firing of a cannon from an ancient port of the Castle, its massive walls suddenly burst into a blaze of light, "from turret to foundation stone." This was taken up by the other castles along the heights and by the bridges and the boats in the river, until one was dazzled by the flash of rockets, and the general rejoicing and confusion.

We had been fortunate in passing up the Rhine valley in the midst of the harvest season; we thus had an opportunity to observe the peasant class at work.

A number of harvest laborers came into a station where we were resting; they laid down their harvest implements while they took their glass of beer. These we examined closely, and were surprised to see how primitive and crude they were as compared with ours in America.

Their hay forks were simply a forked stick cut from the woods; their cradles had a short blade, such as we call a "brier scythe," and also very short fingers; their flails, which they also carried, had a handle as long as a fork handle, and the flail end was about three inches thick with square corners. Such are the harvest implements that can be seen in this age in enlightened Germany.

While passing through Baden, we noticed that the peasants very often work their cows for oxen, but use no yokes. The cattle pull altogether by their heads by straps fastened under their horns. In this way they pull in a line with their spinal column, and seem to draw light loads with more ease than do ours with the yoke and bow, which latter often twists and chokes the steer. In Italy, on the Campagna one sees them plowing with their buffalo oxen, four abreast, one yoke extending over all.

In Europe one sees no fences on the farm lands; wood is scarce, and even iron cross-ties are coming in use on the railroads. In our country the fences are said to cost more than all the dwellings and other buildings of every description.

To-day in Lucerne we have spent the greater part of the time in walking on the banks of the beautiful lake, and gazing on the snow-capped mountains almost with awe, the prospect is so enchanting.

Of course we visited the "Lion of Thorwaldsen"—hewn in the face of the solid rock, lies stretched in the agonies of death a dying lion, a broken spear piercing his side. This great work of the sculptor commemorates the Swiss soldiers, who laid down their lives to defend Louis XVI of France, 1792. They are commonly known as the "Swiss Guard," and eight hundred perished in their endeavor to defend the Tuileries and that ill-starred monarch. Above the sculpture is carved in the rock the Latin legend: "*Helveti-orum fidei virtuti*," (The faith and valor of Switzerland!)

This reminds us that we passed yesterday through Sempach, in the battle at which place Arnold von Winkelried broke through the Austrian phalanx, and "thus made way for liberty."

At Stanz, seven miles from Lucerne, the native place of this hero, on each anniversary of the battle, there is a grand festival and a gathering of the mountaineers from all the surrounding country—"For what avail the plow or sail, or land or life if freedom fail?" Stanz is also the place where Pestalozzi, the great Swiss teacher and educational reformer, first established his school.

From Lucerne we went to the top of the "Rhigi Kulm," one of the noted, isolated peaks of the Alps. Here is a fine hotel, where we passed the night, but were aroused at half-past three in the morning to view the sunrise from this great height. The Alpine horn echoed loud and long, before the sleepy travellers could be awakened from their slumbers; but it was well worth their while, for the day broke fair, and the sunrise scene of the gilded mountain peaks, and the glaciers were grand and beautiful beyond expression. The prospect from this mountain embraces a circuit of three hundred miles.

The peasant girls here sold the rare eidelweiss flower to the travelers: they are not found on this mountain, but are brought by the guides from near the snow line of the tallest peaks.

We descended the mountain by the railroad which is built on what is called "the rack and pinion system"—that is there are three rails with a cog-wheel that works under the locomotive and on the center rail. The locomotive is always placed below the passenger car, and only one car is taken at a time, as the gradient is one foot in four at the steepest point.

We took the steamboat at Vitznaw, bound for Fluelen at the foot of the lake. From Fluelen to Milan, through the heart of the Alps, we passed through fifty-six tunnels and traveled twenty-five and a half miles under ground. The St. Gotthard tunnel proper, is nine and a half miles long—a mile or two longer than the Mont Cenis tunnel. Here, on the St. Gotthard, the head springs of the Rhine, the Rhone and the Inn are within a stone's throw of each other.

Lucerne is called the "Lake of the Four Forest Cantons" and the magnificence of its scenery, perhaps, is not surpassed in any country. Many places upon its beautiful banks are associated with noted events and traditions of Switzerland in her long struggle to maintain freedom.

VENICE.

We arrived in ancient Venice two days ago, and in the picturesque gondolas have floated up and down the Grand Canal and through many a winding way, looking upon the architectural display of buildings whose glory has departed; but beauty still is here where "the sprinkled isles, lily on lily, o'erlace the sea."

Magnificent palaces, adorned exteriorly by sculptures of most eminent artists, line these canals; they are now time-stained and falling to decay. Venice, we are told, is on eighty islands, and has one hundred and forty seven canals; the Grand Canal being two miles long, winding in serpentine fashion through the city. This is the objective point of visitors and people of all races and countries are here to be seen.

At the time of our arrival a great gondola race had just closed and we had an opportunity to see gondoliers in their gala-day costumes, blue, white, green, with orange and golden sashes, and their oriental caps, swarthy features, and dark, curly locks, lithe and graceful figures—they presented an appearance graceful in the

107

extreme as they stood erect upon their beautiful boats and with long sweeps of the oar sent them rapidly through the water.

The Grand Canal has been called by some one the greatest street in the world; it must certainly be the strangest thoroughfare of all the earth!

In going to our hotel, "The Beau Rivage," we passed under the Rialto bridge, and also the *Ponte dei Sospiri*, or "Bridge of Sighs," which latter, Howells, the American writer, calls "a pathetic swindle." This bridge led from the criminal courts in the palace to the dungeons on the opposite side of the canal; it was here that Byron stood at midnight with "a palace and a prison on either hand."

We went down into the prisons which are dismal and awful in every detail; here we entered "the cell of the condemned," where prisoners are kept for a few hours before execution. This cell contained a loose stone that might be used for a pillow, and that was all; on this stone the condemned man might lay his head and sleep upon the granite floor, if sleep then could come to him.

In the narrow passage leading to this room was a scant, barred window, after passing which the prisoner was never again permitted to see the light of the earth. The guide informed us that now there were about three hundred criminals in these prisons but none in the condemned cell.

For nearly eleven hundred years Venice was governed by the Doges, and she was the ruler not only of the Adriatic, but her fleets controlled all the Mediterranean waters.

Ruskin called Venice, as viewed by moonlight, "a golden city paved with emerald." Its long and wonderful history is written in the sculptures and paintings that adorn its walls, wrought by the master hands of Titian, Tintoretto, Paul Veronese and Canova.

This is still one of the most religious cities of Italy, and in these gorgeous churches prayer never ceases, night or day.

In the square of St. Mark, surrounded by the church of St. Mark, the Doges' palace, the Kings' palace and the Campanile, the beauty and fashion of the city congregate at night to see and be seen.

Here on the night of our arrival we walked along among the varied throng and listened to the soft and pleasant sound of the Venetian dialect. The scene was strange and attractive to us, being surrounded by more architectural beauty than we have seen in any other city. The sailors with their large ear-rings, the dark-eyed, lithesome girls with their queenly step, the strange music, and the courteous and joyous bearing of all the vast throng, made a charming picture.

We visited St. Marks Church in the morning, and wandered through the great rooms of the

Doges' palace, and gazed upon the glorious masters, until our eyes when closed at night could still see pictures.

There is one feature about these paintings and frescoes that seems astonishing. They are as fresh and bright to-day as if the artist had painted them yesterday. This is accounted for by the fact that this is the only city in the world where there are no horses and streets and no dust; and here the paintings of the old masters are fresher and brighter than in other cities.

We visited the "Church of the Frari" which may be called the Pantheon of Venice, as many of her gifted sons are here buried, while some of their best works adorn the church. Titian and Canova are buried here under monuments of such exquisite workmanship as to be worthy of their genius.

We saw in the Library of the "Doges' palace" the "Golden Book" in which are recorded the coats of arms, and the pedigrees of the Doges, and viewed an autograph letter of Gallileo, and the writing of Dante. Then we were compelled to take our departure from this strange, unique city of the sea.

ROME.

"The hand that rounded Peter's dome,
And groined the aisles of Christian Rome,
Wrought in sad sincerity.
Himself from God he could not free;
He builded better than he knew:
The conscious stone to beauty grew."

Rome, August 5, 1892.

Yesterday, we visited St. Peter's, traversed its immense nave and aisles, and gazed with wonder upon its stupendous dimensions and with admiration upon the works of Bramante and Michael Angelo.

It seems as if heaven had endowed Angelo with gifts supernatural; at once architect, painter, poet, sculptor, and in each excelling the best of the best.

We are told, three hundred and fifty years passed away and forty-three Popes reigned during the time from the commencement of St. Peters to its completion. It is now the largest church in the world. The ceiling of the Sistine Chapel is regarded as the culminating effort of modern art, and none but the master hand of Michael Angelo, a painter in architectural effects without peer, could have produced the life-

like figures that stand forth on these walls, the
admiration of pilgrims from every country.

"The best prophet of the future is the past;"
then what lessons are to be read here in Rome
—in marble, in bronze, in painting, and in her
vast ruins. Those who can read—may read in
the bas-reliefs on the columns of Trajan and
Antoninus the history of their times and deeds
as plainly as the day on which they were written.

Last night we drove to the Colosseum and
walked alone through its gigantic arches. The
moon was shining, making golden bands across
the dark shadows and all was silent, as we were
the only ones within the vast ruins where in the
olden times 87,000 spectators had applauded
the contests of gladiators and wild beasts. If
these mighty walls could repeat the sounds they
have echoed, the darkest page in history could
be written.

In the days of Augustus, the "Imperial" city
must have numbered two millions of people;
some historians claim that it then contained
seven million.

We saw to-day the marble font in which
Constantine the Great, the first Christian emperor of Rome, was baptized; also, the marble
slab on which Charlemagne stood when he was
crowned emperor.

And here lived Virgil, "that landscape lover,

lord of language;" and Cicero, the orator and great master of composition; and Livy with his wonderful powers of description; and Tasso, the epic poet; and Tacitus, the historian, with his profound insight into the dark recesses of human conduct; all were here and have passed away.

Rome since the consolidation of the kingdom has made rapid strides in modern improvements and may still be considered one of the beautiful cities of the world. Its streets, public squares, churches, palaces, and multitudes of public buildings, built in a style of elegance and solidity; its obelisks and columns, its fountains decorated with artistic taste, dispensing pure water to every part of the city; and its master pieces of scientific painting and architecture, ancient and modern, together with its delightful climate—present a picture so vast and varied that it may still be regarded as one of the most interesting cities of the world. And of "Rome the lone mother of dead empires," the lines of Propertius, the elegiac poet, may still be appropriate:

"*Omnia Romanae cedant, miraculae terrae,*
Natura hic potuit, quidquid ubique fecit."

In our brief intercourse with them we have been pleased with the citizens; they are very courteous and of a grave, thoughtful demeanor. They seem to be fond of music and street parades, and of spectacles; and all this we know, descends to them as natural heirs, when we recall the pageants of ancient times, when Rome collected here the spoils of conquered nations; and when her conquerors, such as Pompey the Great, marched three hundred captive princes before his triumphal car.

We visited to-day the Convent of the Capuchin Friars and saw a number of rooms adorned—if that word may be properly used in such a connection—with the bones of their dead monks!

Jaw bones were arranged together; tibulas, fibulas, pelvis bones, skulls, heads of femurs, ribs, scapulas and various bones of the body were thus classified, and arranged in bunches of flowers; center pieces, border pieces, and numerous forms, very like ornamental shell work! It was a gruesome sight and the ladies would fain have avoided it. This afternoon we drove four miles outside the city, along the famous Appian Way. A mile from the walls of the city we came to the church called, "*Domine Quo Vadis*," because as tradition has it, when Peter the Apostle was driven from the city through persecution—when he had arrived at this spot he here met the Saviour bearing the Cross—and said to him— "*O Domine Quo Vadis?*" In proof of this tradition, the foot-print of the naked foot of the Savior is still to be seen in the marble of the old pathway of the Appian Way! Here it was that the church referred to was built.

We pursued our journey along this road, viewing the tombs of those who had been great and powerful in their day; for it was such as these alone, who were honored with a tomb along the Appia. We passed the tomb of Seneca, and approached the site of the villa where Cicero had lived, and then returned to the Church of St. Sebastian. At this point we entered the famous Catacombs of Rome, but we were somewhat disappointed in them.

On Sunday morning we visited the museum and the Capitoline Hill, one of the famous hills on which the "Imperial" city sat, and "from her throne of beauty ruled the world." We looked with much interest on the portrait bust of Julius Cæsar, and also upon that of Brutus, and upon the rare beauty of "Venus of Capitola," and upon many other things, at which we could only glance.

We saw the place at which the infamous Caligula was assassinated, and also that where Rienzi, "the last of the tribunes," fell; and where the envious Casca and Brutus too, stabbed Cæsar, "the noblest Roman of them all."

Ilex trees and gardens now grow on the top of the debris that covers a portion of the Palace of the Cæsars.

Excavations at Rome, of late years, have re-

vealed much of its ancient history.   One of the
guard rooms of Cæsar's Palace was laid bare,
and showed markings on the walls made by the
heathen soldiers who were on duty here, so many
centuries ago.   Now, it is evident from the
writings on these walls that there were Chris-
tians among the soldiers of Tiberius; it is also
made apparent that they were persecuted and
derided by their heathen comrades-in-arms.   On
the wall of the guard room of Tiberius was
found the first representation of the Crucifixion
that was, perhaps, ever made.

   It was made by one of these barbarian soldiers
with his spear or some other sharp implement—
traced in the plaster, there to remain, and to be
uncovered from the debris nearly two thousand
years later.   This drawing consists of the figure
of a man's body with an ass' head suspended
upon a cross.   Underneath is written in ancient
Greek, the inscription: "This is the God of
Alexamenos!" Later there was unearthed, in
the adjoining room, the reply of Alexamenus to
his persecutor.   There was found a cross, most
carefully drawn, and a figure kneeling before it
in a devout attitude.   Underneath was written
the legend in Latin: *"Alexamenes fidelis,"*
Alexamenus the faithful!

   It is a curious circumstance that the first picture of the Crucifixion is this crude drawing,
made by a heathen in sacrilegious derision!

On the day of our departure we left Rome at one o'clock for Naples, and arrived there a little before seven p. m. Until about three o'clock the heat was intense, and the country we passed through was barren and desolate in the extreme; but as we approached Naples, where the land had been irrigated, there were fair crops of corn, and also of bamboo and hemp. We saw Vesuvius smoking in the distance, but there was no fire issuing from its crater.

POMPEII.

On our way to Pompeii we crossed the bay to Capri, which island is distant fourteen miles from Naples. The morning was fair and the sky blue, and the Bay of Naples seemed worthy of all the praise that has ever been lavished upon it. Before leaving the anchorage some swarthy divers came around the vessel, and gave us an exhibition of their skill in diving to great depths to recover the coins the passengers tossed into the water.

Our sail across the bay to Capri was one of perfect enjoyment, and to those unfamiliar with the scene, it was as if they sailed on enchanted waters. The rocky sides of Capri are terraced, and it is planted with olive trees and grape vines. Here we went in the small boats and entered a strange, weird cavern called, "The Blue Grotto." The entrance is low and narrow and can only be entered when the sea is calm. Visitors from afar come to view the strange beauties of this cavern, which are, perhaps, produced by the deep blue cast of the water, which in turn is produced by the deep blue of the sky; another peculiar effect is produced by the phosphorescent quality of the water—for the divers swimming here seem as molten images—every limb in motion—as if made of living fire. The effect is startling.

Tiberius, that imperious emperor, lived on this island in the latter years of his life, and a small cliff is pointed out which is called "Tiberius' Leap;" for from this point he caused slaves to be thrown over to their destruction, merely that he might witness their anguish and terror, in the face of death!

We sailed from Capri to Sorrento where we left the vessel; this town is built upon a tall cliff, from which, it is said, one has the finest view that can be obtained of the Bay of Naples. This is the birth-place of Tasso, and a fine monuments tands here to his memory. The streets are mean and narrow, but several fine hotels crown the heights overlooking the bay: these are resorted to by many summer visitors. At the time of our visit this place was the residence of F. Marion Crawford, the novelist.

We drove from Capri, fifteen miles around the bay, to Pompeii; the day was intensely hot at the time, and we suffered very much from the heat.

At Pompeii we viewed the things that have been so often described, and also some new objects of interest that had just been unearthed. We found a small number of workmen, men and boys, digging in a room lately discovered: they

used light picks and shovels and baskets to remove the ashes that had belched forth from the
volcano of Vesuvius in the year '79 and enveloped and buried the place.

All the houses are one story, some of them
beautifully adorned with frescoed walls, columns
and tile flooring. This was a fashionable resort
of the wealthy Roman people, and here they had
their summer residences.

We removed with our cane the ashes from the
side of a column in the house where we found
the men and boys at work. We dug down for
two or three feet for the ashes were very light
and easily moved. We were astonished to find
the fresco painting on this column as bright
and fresh as if it had just been finished, although
it had not seen the light of day for 1800 years!

On the wall of the room, from which the
workmen had just removed the ashes, we saw
the drawing of a ship that had been cut in the
plaster with a knife, apparently from its height,
done by a boy or some person of low stature;
there it remained, plain and fresh, a very good
representation of a craft still seen on these waters—drawn by some boy nearly two thousand
years ago!

Casts of the bodies that have perished here
are obtained in the following manner: the ex-
plorer probes about with an iron rod in the debris until a hollow place is found; from

this he removes the rod and into the hole pours
a solution of plaster of paris, and when it is set
the ashes are removed. In this way an exact
cast is made of the body that has decayed and
left its mold in the pumice stone that enveloped
the doomed city.

These are most ghastly and lifelike images,
exactly true in their minutest detail; and it is
pitiful—the expressions of pain and horror de-
picted upon the countenances of those who perished here.

Our best knowledge of ancient painting before
the Christian era is obtained from Pompeii, and
the better class of houses are adorned with very
beautiful mosaic pavements.

The buried site of this ancient town, lying
beneath the vineyards and mulberry grounds,
was accidentally discovered by a peasant in digging a well, in the year 1748. Excavations have
been made here in a small way continuously
since that time. Now about one third of Pompeii is uncovered, and on the remaining portion
grow Indian corn and other crops.

By this discovery a flood of light has been
thrown upon ancient life, in all its details, so
that we may picture to ourselves the habits,
manners and customs of those who lived here; a
knowledge more accurate and minute than can
be obtained from ancient literature.

In the "Museo Borbonico," in Naples, we

viewed the most important relics taken from the buried city; household utensils, surgical instruments, mechanical tools, paintings and statuary, rings and cameos, and jewelry of exquisite workmanship—all tending to show that those who lived here two thousand years ago were scarcely inferior to this age in the comforts and refinements of life.

THE MIDWAY PLAISANCE.

Some one has made an estimate of the time it would take to see the World's Fair in detail if two minutes were given to each exhibit, and he concludes that it could be done in thirty-two years. This is probably incorrect and an under statement of the facts; at least no sane person would attempt to gain a comprehensive knowledge of the Fair in that way. We propose to write merely a few notes, taken daily, in passing through the "Midway Plaisance," but of the Fair proper, only a few sentences of general impressions.

We saw a stalwart Texan, with all the insouciance of his kind, walk into the Midway Plaisance. He had just come from the bewilderment of the "White City," and his thoughts were doubtless still in that dreamland. But he had not gone far before his listless air vanished and he stood agape at the fantastic scenes presented in this pleasure ground of the barbaric nations.

The student of human nature is edified even in observing children at play, as there is gained a knowledge of temperament, natural aptitude, and an insight into individual traits. And here are the children of nature, the uncivilized races, and the semi-civilized races, those interesting types of mankind, some of whom not so long ago would have eaten the sightseers with the same relish with which they ate of the blubber of the sea-horse! This is not a pleasant reflection, yet we shall observe these foreign folks with no less interest on that account, even if we do note with feelings of some aversion the strong white teeth of the dusky cannibal race who may have employed them in eating human flesh in the recent past.

It happened that we stopped at the Lapp Village among the first places visited. The Laplanders are short of stature; the average man is five feet, and the women about four feet. They are of a dingy, pale color, weak-eyed, broad-mouthed, and appear strong and stupid. They have their huts which they brought with them across the water. Here one may study their every-day life, which is interesting as showing the struggle for existence in their inhospitable country. They have their sleds, snow shoes, and one reindeer which is all that is left of thirteen they brought a few weeks since from Lapland. The climate of Chicago has proven fatal to the reindeer accustomed to sniff the air of the North Cape. The king of the Lapps, a stolid old man, is here. His name is "King Bull," and it is said that he owns three thousand reindeer, which would make his fortune about fifty thousand dollars, but to use a colloquial expression, "he does not look it."

From Lapland we went to Switzerland, which is a long distance to travel within the space of a few minutes. Here we saw the panorama of the Swiss Alps, the glaciers, moraines, and snow covered peaks. Far down in the valley was heard the alpine horn, and the chamois were seen scaling the dangerous path; and by looking closely one could detect the meager flora of those heights, and even the rare edelweiss, the queen flower of the Alps. As the gloom of night fell, lights shone from cottage windows whence issued the sounds of voices singing the mountain songs, dear to the Switzer's heart. The whole scene was natural and lifelike.

As electricity is the special study of this age, and the science now being developed, we were induced to visit next in the "Midway," "The Electric Scenic Theatre." Here electricity is used to produce landscape effects, shades, shadows and perspective with marvelous accuracy. We had studied for some time in the Electric Building of the World's Fair, but of this we cannot at present speak; our task is limited to the "Plaisance," and besides, we must not be drawn by the fascinations of science from the more interesting study of man, though it is of man of the lower types; he has still that vital spark,

that torch of humanity, which will glow when
the wheels of all machines have stopped, and
the hum of industry is silent.

In the streets of old Cairo one soon forgets
such reflections, and enters into the spirit of the
place, which sets one back two hundred years
from this year of grace. One familiar with
that city has said: "This street is more like old
Cairo than Cairo itself." The houses, the Arabs,
the Fellahs, the donkeys, the camels and the
venders are the same; but the fair American
girls who ride on the donkeys and camels in the
Cairo streets of the Midway, differ from the
dark, veiled women of the Nile, more than the
lily differs from the sunflower. This is perhaps
the most popular place in the Plaisance, if not
the most instructive; yet what does one care for
instruction, when all is life, bustle and jollity,
and the gay jest and the jocund laugh are
heard, as the women and children ride by on
camels and donkeys, driven by Arab boys who
call out, "like up!" meaning "look out," as
they drive the ungainly camel through the
crowded streets. The *tout ensemble* of the scene
is oriental and strange to western eyes.

On leaving the fair grounds proper, just to
the right as you enter the "Midway" is the international beauty show, veiled under the modest title, "The International Dress Costume
Co." One conjures up visions of statuesque

Circassians, and Houri from Mingrelia; and
enters expecting these illusions to be dispelled,
but not so! for here are as fair types as one
could see in a journey around the world. The
young men of the party, who have keen taste
in such matters, awarded the mead of beauty to
the English girl, and next in order as named:
the Scotch, Welch, Polish, Greek, and so on. A
dark girl from Syria was an interesting type.

A reporter was questioning the Scotch "lassie," as we passed, and she replied in low, sweet
tones: "Everything is very grand and fine here
in America, but I wad nae live here alway, sir;
I am frae Caithness." Her cheeks flushed and
she showed emotion, as she spoke of her home,
and it was easy to see that her heart was still
in the Highlands.

The costumes of these girls from the different
nations were in many instances very picturesque; they represented about thirty nationalities. A girl from Paris displayed one of Worth's
finest costumes; yet some of the others, in their
simple, native dress, adorning modest beauty,
were more attractive.

If time would permit we should write of many
more scenes witnessed in this pleasure ground of
nations. Here is the place to study character
and to gain a knowledge of the strange people
of the earth.

Of the World's Fair proper, books will be

written and the influence that will radiate from here will set the world forward at least a generation in arts, science, and learning and all that pertains to the welfare of man.

It is impossible through mere words for the mind to form any adequate conception of scenes of such magnitude and splendor. But the glorious vision of this incomparable "White City," with its noble facades and clustered spires, upreared to the sky, once pictured on the retina in youth will live in the memory till the eyes have grown dim to the fading light of the world.

In the old Bible days, Philip came and announced to Nathaniel the happening of the most hopeful and amazing event that ever affected human destiny; but he doubting that such things could be as narrated by Philip, that apostle simply replied: "Come and see."

AUDUBON AND THE BIRDS.

John James Audubon, an American ornithologist of great eminence, was born in Louisiana in the year 1780. He was the son of a French naval officer who had settled as a planter in that state. When very young he had a passion for observing the habits of birds: he made many sketches of them and disclosed considerable talent as a draughtsman. He was sent to Paris to be educated and studied design in the school of David, the first painter under Napoleon the Great, and especially distinguished for his draughtsmanship.

Audubon proved himself worthy of such a master, and on his return to his native country two years later he settled on the banks of the Schuylkill, in Pennsylvania, where he owned a farm. Here he passed ten years of his life in researches into the habits of birds, in his drawings of them and in painting them by hand in lifelike colors. It was during these years that he laid the foundation of the great work which he afterward produced.

However, it was fated that he was not to use the material here collected, for a great trial

now befell him when, after having accumulated
a large stock of the most carefully executed designs, he discovered that the whole of them had
been destroyed by mice. This was a greater
disaster than the fabled loss of Newton's scientific manuscript; for while that was a mere
tradition, the loss of Audubon was real and almost irreparable. Yet he possessed that extra-
ordinary strength of mind that enabled him to
view his loss with serenity, and to patiently
begin again the work of years.

He moved to Henderson on the Ohio River,
where he lived for several years with his wife and
children. He now commenced a series of excur-
sions through the vast, primeval forest which he
explored alone, and in which he passed the
greater portion of his time for many years. He
produced colored designs of all the birds he
could find, being impelled to this pursuit by his
love of nature, rather than an ambition to make
himself famous.

In 1826 he went to England, and in London
began the publication of his great work, "The
Birds of America." He was everywhere received
by learned societies and scientific men with the
utmost cordiality and enthusiasm. Among his
warmest admirers in Great Britain were Sir
Walter Scott, Francis Jeffrey and John Wilson;
and in Paris, Cuvier, St. Hiliaire, Humbolt, and
other savants.

He obtained a hundred subscribers to his magnificent work at one thousand dollars a copy. It was in folio, illustrated with about four hundred and forty-eight plates of one thousand and sixty-five species of birds of natural size, beautifully colored. It consists of five volumes of engravings, designed by himself, and five volumes of letter press.

The French naturalist Cuvier, who was himself accounted as "the father of comparative anatomy," said of Audubon's "Birds of America:" "It is the most magnificent monument that art has ever erected to ornithology." This work cannot be purchased now at any price.

After Audubon returned to America he explored the coasts, the lakes, the rivers and the mountains, from Labrador and Canada to Florida. He crossed the ocean several times after this and lived to prepare smaller editions to his great work, and also a work on quadrupeds.

To an excellent skill in designing natural objects, he added an admirable talent for describing them in graphic language.

His character is thus eulogized by Prof. Wilson of the Edinburg University.

"The hearts of all warmed toward Audubon who were capable of conceiving the difficulties, dangers and sacrifices that must have been encountered, endured and overcome, before genius could have embodied these, the glory of its

innumerable triumphs.   The man himself is just
what you would expect from his production,
full of fine enthusiasm and intelligence, most
interesting in looks and manners, a perfect gentleman, and esteemed by all who know him for
the simplicity and frankness of his nature.   He
is the greatest artist in his own walk that has
ever lived."

It is interesting to note that the favorite bird
of this great master was the wood-thrush.   This
small brown bird is but little known except to
those familiar with the woods.   It is shy and
retiring, frequenting thick woods and tangled
undergrowth.   Its form is stout, the general
color is rufous brown above, lighter on the head,
pure white below, with numerous blackish spots
on breast and sides.   It is smaller than either
the robin or the brown thrush.   The nest is
placed in a bush or the fork of a sapling—very
often a dogwood—and is constructed without
mud; the eggs are from four to six and of a
greenish blue color.

The wood-thrush is the last bird heard at
night and the first at the dawn of day.   When
the first rays of dawn penetrate the gloomy recesses of the forest aisles, its powerful, clear and
mellow notes break upon the silence, rising and
falling in gentle cadence.   Its notes are few,
yet they are very pleasing.

"The song of the wood-thrush thrills sweet through
        the wood.
So flute-like and clear, the ecstatic prelude."

In "Doddridge's Notes," which are regarded
as original authority relating to the pioneer history of West Virginia, the author says: "The
crow and the blackbird and the great variety of
singing birds were not natives of the primeval forests, but followed in the path of emigration."

Now in the fields and groves are found all the
species known to this latitude, there being over
forty varieties of the warbler family alone. These
birds are now "native and to the manner born,"
and it were better to study them in the woods
and the fields than to read about strange birds
of distant countries that we may never see, and
whose songs may never add to our enjoyment.
The same is true of the study of the flowers, the
plants and the trees that are before us in the
book of nature.

Observation is the basis of original thought,
and the youth who acquires a habit of atten-
tively observing objects of nature will grow in
this knowledge, unlearned of books, as he grows
in stature. He will learn to give heed to the
songs of birds and his ear will become attuned
to the sounds of the field and the forest. His
eye will detect the changing hues of the sky,
the tiny flower, the majestic tree and the beauty
in all things will brighten and cheer his pathway.

But the world must ever appear as different to individuals as their minds are diverse. To one it will always be a narrow place, paved with hard dollars, with but little of the blue sky above; to another mind it must remain a wonderful if not a pleasant world; for the whole globe, men and things, and the vicissitudes of life will lie within the power of its comprehension.

But these are the extremes; the masses of humanity trudge between the two in devious paths, with unequal knowledge and with unequal powers of enjoying the gifts of the Creator.

THE 22ND DAY OF FEBRUARY.

REFLECTIONS UPON WASHINGTON.

General Washington owned 10,000 acres of land in one body at Mt. Vernon, which he farmed upon a very large scale, especially for that day. Here he employed 250 hands and kept 24 plows going all the year, when the weather would permit. In the year 1787 he sowed 600 bushels of oats and 700 acres of wheat, besides other crops. At that time he had 140 horses, 112 cows and other stock in proportion. He rode around his farm every day unless the weather was very stormy, and he was constantly making various and extensive experiments for the improvement of agriculture. He said that he loved the retirement of his home above all things and that it was with regret that he left it to assume the command of the army or to take the presidential chair.

All contemporary accounts agree that Washington was a man of dignified and imposing presence. He was six feet, two inches in height; the muscular development of his form was perfect, and he never at any period of his life became too stout for easy and graceful move-

135

ments.   Custis says: "His complexion was fair
but considerably florid."   His hair was brown,
his eyes blue.   He was scrupulously attentive to
the proprieties of dress and personal appearance;
his manner was gracious and gentle; yet he was
a diffident man, and always maintained a certain
military reserve when in public.   He was a fearless and skillful horseman, and rode to the
hounds with the keen zest of a sportsman.

Washington was forty-three years of age
when appointed by the Continental Congress to
command the army of the Revolution.   It has
been somewhat the custom in modern times to
decry his military ability; but this is done
chiefly by those "who never set a squadron in
the field," nor looked upon the storm of battle.
The "elements were so mixed in him," and such
was the admirable equipoise of all his faculties
that he was perhaps, in practical wisdom, the
peer of any man that ever lived.

In the light of history, in looking back now
at the events of the Revolution, we can but
believe if any one of our ablest generals, such
as Green, Wayne, Morgan or Gates had been in
chief command, that the raw, undisciplined
forces of the Continentals would have been
crushed by the well-drilled regulars of the British on the plains of New Jersey, if not before
that time.   Washington well knew the character of each army, both of officers and men, and

he knew that it would be necessary to act on the defensive, and to husband all the resources of his little army, otherwise there could be no hope for the cause of liberty.

Neither public clamor nor gross abuse, nor the calls of ambition, could divert him from his steady purpose, nor cause him to make with his army one rash or ill-considered maneuver. He possessed enterprise and prudence, and in his tact and forbearance in dealing with men, he has had no superior among our modern generals.

It was barely possible for the Continental army to gain the victory through the patient, long drawn struggle of eight years; but it would have been impossible for it to have been successful had it faced the British regulars in open, decisive battles, especially in the earlier part of the war. By the latter method the Continental troops would have been decimated and scattered and the liberty of this country would have perished with them.

By pursuing a safe and patient course, Washington, with his ragged Continentals, was enabled for eight years to confront the armies of Great Britain, and through his indomitable courage and wisdom, he prevailed against his powerful adversary and finally succeeded in planting the tree of liberty on this soil, where now its branches overspread the continent.

In remembrance of our obligations, it is a sacred duty to commemorate the birthday of this illustrious man, and in every country where oppressed men are struggling for freedom they find inspiration and hope in the glorious example of Washington.

At the close of his farewell address, which was in times past the Palladium of our elder, if not abler statesmen, he says with pathetic earnestness: "In offering you, my countrymen, these counsels of an old and affectionate friend, I dare not hope that they will make the strong and lasting impression I could wish: that they will control the usual current of the passions, or prevent our nation from running the course which has hitherto marked the destiny of nations; but if I may even flatter myself that they may be productive of some partial benefit, some occasional good, that they may now and then recur to moderate the fury of party spirit, to warn against the importunities of pretended patriotism, this hope will be a full recompense for the solicitude for your welfare, by which they have been dictated."

In speaking of the unconscious errors he may have committed, he continues; "Whatever they may be I fervently beseech the Almighty to avert or mitigate the evils to which they may tend. I shall carry with me the hope that my country will never cease to view them with indulgence;

and that after forty-five years of my life dedicated to its service with an upright zeal, the faults of incompetent abilities will be consigned to oblivion, as myself must soon be to the mansions of rest."

AN HISTORICAL SKETCH.

GEN. GEORGE ROGERS CLARK.

The local records of the town of Clarksburg, W. Va., show that at an early meeting of the settlers at this place, the name for the town was suggested and adopted, in honor of Gen. Clark. This meeting was held sometime prior to October 1785, for it was then that the town was incorporated.

This was probably the first public recognition of the services of this able officer, who had wrested the Northwest Territory from the British and Indians, and had held it against all odds, under circumstances of peculiar hardships, and as it proved in the end, at the sacrifice of his personal fortun e.

It is a regrettable circumstance that our modern historians have almost ignored the services of Gen. Clark. He was doubtless, in a military point of view, one of the most accomplished and useful officers that served on the western frontier in the war of the Revolution.

It is seldom that a military officer whose services have redounded in results of such vast importance to his country, has gone to his grave

140

unrewarded and forgotten, save, perhaps, by the descendants of the hardy pioneers who shared with him the toils and dangers of the border warfare.

Until quite recently, one was compelled to search the original writings of pioneer times in order to give even a brief sketch of his life.

George Rogers Clark was born near Charlottesville, Virginia, in 1752. In early life he was a farmer and a surveyor. He first appeared upon the scene of public action, as a captain in Dunmore's War; but further than this we have been unable to learn any particulars of him at this period.

Upon the breaking out of the Revolution, he soon became distinguished as one of the most active leaders of the frontiersmen, in their heroic efforts to protect the border settlements from the incursion of the Indians. Patriotism and a laudable desire for military fame seem to have been the predominant traits of his character. He rallied the backwoodsmen at points of danger; led counter attacks against the Indians; built block-houses and forts, and, although quite a young man, displayed such great courage, firmness and military skill in all these exploits, that whenever he appeared upon the border, he was the acknowledged leader of the backwoodsmen.

He led through the wilderness the party of pioneers who made the first settlement at the falls of the Ohio river, where the city of Louisville now stands, and he was its able defender during the subsequent years of savage warfare.

Before leaving the immediate border of Virginia, however, he is said to have made the plan for Fort Henry at Wheeling; and which afterwards withstood several fierce assaults, and one four-days siege from the Indians. It was here that Elizabeth Zane performed that valorous act which has been celebrated by the painter and the poet; but as Kipling says, "that is another story."

In June 1775, a meeting of the settlers of Kentucky known as, "The Dark and Bloody ground," and then a part of Virginia, took place at Harrodstown. Their object was to secure the aid of the Commonwealth in defense of their homes. They selected Clark and one other to represent them before the General Assembly then in session at Williamsburg, the capital of the state.

Clark and his companion started upon their long journey through the unbroken wilderness; but when after many days they reached Fincastle, they learned to their regret, that the Assembly had adjourned.

Clark's companion then returned to the woods, but he himself proceeded to the residence of Governor Patrick Henry in Hanover County. He found the Governor lying sick at home, but he listened with interest while Clark explained the object of his journey.

This soldier from the woods, at the same time made known to the Governor the bold and daring scheme he had formed for the reduction of the British posts in the Illinois country. Clark found in Governor Henry a man of similar spirit to his own; he cordially approved the hazardous plans he had formed, and gave him a letter to that effect, directed to the Council of State. Clark appeared before that body and presented his petition in August 1776. He received from the authorities an order for five hundred pounds of powder to be delivered to him at Ft. Pitt. He at the same time received a colonel's commission with a warrant to raise a regiment, and was ordered to protect the settlers in Kentucky.

These were orders from the state authorities that were made public; but he had induced them through his appeals, and by the sanction of Governor Henry, to give him the secret order to attack the British post of Kaskaskia in the Illinois country. This last order Clark did not divulge to his officers and men for many weeks, not until the opportune moment had arrived for its execution.

It appears that Clark's Expedition started down the Ohio river from "Red Stone Old Fort," with only three companies, which had been recruited in the counties of Fauquier, Frederick, and the country west of the Blue Ridge.

When his boats had arrived at the mouth of the Great Kanawha, he found that the post there had been attacked the day before by the savages; and because he would not stop to pursue them, he received censure from those who did not know of his more important plans.

Floating day after day with the current, the expedition finally reached the Falls of the Ohio where Fort Jefferson was erected. Here Clark received some reinforcements, which increased his command to four companies, less than four hundred men.

Col. Clark then announced to his officers and men the true object of the expedition, and on June 24, 1778, his boats passed the Falls of the Ohio, and the expedition was fairly launched that was destined to change the boundary line of the nation.

When the boats had reached a point not far from the mouth of the Wabash, Col. Clark landed with a part of his command; he ordered the others to proceed with the boats and the baggage to the mouth of the Ohio, and thence to Kaskaskia on the river of that name, one mile east of the Mississippi.

He then marched across the country by the most direct route for the same place. When he emerged from the woods in sight of the village of Kaskaskia, the inhabitants were as surprised as if he had dropped from the clouds. He took the precaution to march his men in a circuitous manner past an opening in the timber which led the enemy to count them two or three times without discovering the artifice.

Then with a part of his men he advanced against the fort with his flag displayed, and sternly demanded the unconditional surrender of the garrison.

Rocheblave, the commandant of the fort, dismayed at the sudden apparition of an armed force, dropped upon him from the clouds as it were, and with an exaggerated idea of the force of his enemy, surrendered at discretion.

Col. Clark then proceeded as rapidly as possible to the British post of Cahokia, about sixty miles north of Kaskaskia and four miles south of the present site of East St. Louis. Here also he succeeded in capturing this garrison without bloodshed.

These conquests were achieved before the arrival of the main body of his forces from the boats, and were made known through spies to the British Governor, Hamilton, of Detroit, then at the post of Vincennes on the Wabash. Gov. Hamilton was apprised at the same time of the small force by which the forts were captured. He immediately took steps to collect a large force, in order to surprise the Americans, and retake the posts. But before he could accomplish his purpose Col. Clark's reserve arrived at Kaskaskia from the boats; when, leaving a sufficient number to hold the forts he had captured he marched without delay against Ft. St. Vincennes.

This was an arduous march of many days through the swamps and quagmires of the Wabash : the men often wading to their armpits in the ice cold water; yet they did not hesitate to follow their heroic leader. They were five days marching the last nine miles. This was in February 1779, and they must have perished had not the weather been mild for the season.

On the 23rd of February, Col. Clark led his men from the swamps and stood upon the solid ground in front of the fort at Vincennes. The place was taken completely by surprise, and after a siege of eighteen hours the fort was carried by storm.

Governor Hamilton and his whole garrison, numbering more men than Clark had in his command, became prisoners of war. Hamilton, who had incited the savages to deeds of atrocity by paying rewards for human scalps, was sent to Virginia where he was treated as a felon and imprisoned in chains, but was finally exchanged.

Thus within a few months, Col. Clark had gained possession of all the British posts northwest of the Ohio, and had moved the boundary line of Virginia from that river to the Mississippi.

This expedition has been compared in difficulty and suffering, and in daring courage, to
that of the memorable march of Arnold to Quebec in December 1775; but it was far more
important in its results.

Unfortunately, the state of Virginia when it
commissioned Col. Clark to raise a regiment
for the protection of the western frontier, did
not provide means for its support, but author-
ized him to procure supplies as he could, either
on his own credit or on that of the state. Act-
ing upon this authority he at first gave drafts
upon the state of Virginia for supplies for his
army; at the same time he pledged his personal
security for their payment.

On the 2nd of January 1781 the Assembly of
Virginia ceded to the United States the territory northwest of the Ohio river which they had
established in 1778 as the "County of Illinois,"
at the request of Col. Clark for the appointment
of a civil government for the territory he had
conquered.

After this time the state of Virginia claimed
that all expenses incurred by Col. Clark in capturing the Illinois country, and in holding
possession of it, should be assumed by the Government of the United States.

The general Government did not acknowledge
this claim, and Col. Clark was thrown on his
own resources; either to abandon his conquest,

or to hold it. He was an officer equal to the occasion. As his difficulties increased his resolution gained strength, and when the appeals of the state and government had failed, he resolved to hold his conquests by the strong hand of power.

He took by force such scanty supplies as he could do with, for the support of his army, from the sparse population of the country. He gave them in return certified accounts, to be paid by the state of Viriginia or by himself; and as his personal credit at this time was better than that of the state, of course he was the one looked to for payment.

Thus General Clark continued to hold possession of this valuable territory until the close of the Revolution, otherwise the strong grasp of England would have been upon it: and it is safe to say that she would have held yet all the territory included in the States of Ohio, Indiana, Illinois, Michigan and Wisconsin.

The proof of this assertion is attested by the diplomatic correspondence of the Treaty of Paris, signed Sept. 3rd, 1783. Here it is expressly stated that the tenable ground of making the boundary line at the Lakes instead of at the Ohio river, as the British commissioners claimed, was the fact that General Clark had conquered the country and was at that very time in actual military possession of it.

Thus we see that consequences of great import hinged upon the acts of this officer; yet in the American Cyclopædia there is not one line of his biography; although brief mention is made of his brother, William Clark, who was one of the principals in the "Expedition of Lewis & Clark," the first to cross the Rocky Mountains in the year 1804.

The expenses of General Clark's expedition were never paid by his state and not by the government until long after his death. He on his part, honorably sacrificed his own property, as far as it would go, to pay these claims. But after he had exhausted a fine estate in this way, he was still harassed by law suits and by the importunities of poor friends, who had aided his expedition.

Under these circumstances he unfortunately gave way to intemperance; and drank of strong drink as if it contained some oblivious antidote that could dispel sorrow. He died near Louisville, Kentucky, February 18, 1818.

The state of Virginia sent General Clark a sword after he had become old and poor; but he broke it into pieces, exclaiming:

"When Virginia needed a sword, I gave her one. She now sends me a toy. I want bread!"

Judge Burnet, of Cincinnati, in his "Notes on the Northwest Territory," in speaking of General Clark, said: "He had the appearance of a

man born to command, and fitted by nature for
his destiny. His majestic person, strong features
and dignified deportment gave evidence of an
intelligent, resolute mind."

This is the only allusion to his personal
appearance that we have seen. He probably
never visited the site where Clarksburg, his first
namesake, stands; but he was known, personally, to some at least, of the settlers who built
their cabins here, more than a century ago. These
honest, simple minded pioneers no doubt thought
when they gave his name to their rude hamlet,
they would thus perpetuate his fame while that
name should abide. Yet there are few now who
know the origin of the name except those who
read the records of the past; for to those who
do not read, there is no past beyond the memories of their youth.

At the time General Clark was raising troops
for his Illinois Campaign, a company was recruited at Clarksburg by Colonel George Jackson.

This company with the thrift of the times
hewed out their canoes from the forest trees,
and into them they loaded their munitions of
war; consisting mostly of their flint-lock rifles,
bullet-pouches, jerked-venison, dried-beef, and
likely, a rundlet or two of corn-whisky.

These men were no holiday soldiers; of lux-
ury they knew not the name; many of them had
heard the whiz of the Indian bullet, and had

stood with rifle in hand in defense of their cabins when the horrid war-whoop had broken on the stillness of the night in the gloom of the forest.

When all was ready the canoes were loosened, and the little fleet floated on the limpid waters beneath the shade of the great trees. It followed the meanders of the river for many days until Redstone Old Fort, Fort Pitt, and Fort Henry were passed, and finally their boats were moored in the mouth of the Great Kanawha.

At this point for some reason that the records do not explain, the expedition was abandoned, and the volunteers from this section returned to their homes.

An anecdote is told of General Clark which will further illustrate his character. At the treaty of Fort Washington, where Cincinnati now stands, Clark had only seventy men, while the Shawnees appeared at the Council with three hundred warriors.

In the council-room of the log fort, Clark sat at a table, with two or three of his officers. The chief of the Shawnees rose, and after making a boisterous speech placed on the table a belt of white wampum ; and also, to the dismay of the whites, a belt of black wampum ; this latter indicated that he was as ready for war as for peace. At the same time the three hundred warriors applauded their chief by a terrific yell.

General Clark pushed the black wampum off the table, then rising as the savages muttered their indignation, he stamped the belt under his feet, and with a look of stern defiance and a voice of thunder he ordered them to leave the hall. They involuntarily left, and the next day sued for peace.

But the quality which distinguished Gen. Clark above all men of his time, save one, was that statesman-like prescience with which he arrived at a just estimate of the future inestimable value of the northwest territory: as late as the first regular Congress under the Constitution, there were senators who thought that the "western wilderness," as they called it, would never be settled; and they stated that it was not worth the cost of its protection by the goverment!

Washington and Clark, to judge from their acts and words, were the only public men of that day who had any just conception of the value of this territory.

And now, while it is in order to commemorate the deeds of Revolutionary heroes, and societies are organized for that purpose, it is but charitable to predict that the beautiful city of Louisville on the banks of the "Belle Riviere," as the French named the Ohio, will in time erect a monument to George Rogers Clark, her founder and defender in the days when the world was young on these western shores.

EVANGELINE.

(In the Acadian Land, the Scene of Longfellow's Poem.)

A few years since, while traveling with a companion through the maritime provinces of Lower Canada, we were turned aside from our route—drawn by an eager desire to visit a spot made classic by the genius of one of our own poets.

It seems wonderful that the creative imagination and the glowing fancy of the poet can cast a spell of enchantment over a material landscape and through mere power of words to endow it with a glamour that does not fade with the lapse of years, but still illumine the deeds narrated and the scene long after the actors on that scene and the poet who wrote of them have passed from earth.

Little did the English officer, Col. Winslow, think when he delivered to the Acadian peasants the cruel proclamation of his king—and which task he declared—"was painful to his natural make and temper,"—that the events of that day would be perpetuated in the lines of a beautiful poem.

Some such thoughts we had as we left the

158

train at the lonely station of Grand Pré, in Nova
Scotia.

We stood then "In the Acadian Land, on the
shores of the Basin of Minas." Yet, without
the story of Evangeline and the poem, the
scene presented here might not have lived in
our memory; but now every spot was glowing
with the poet's touch.

"Stretching to the eastward," and all around
were "the vast meadows that had given the
name to the village."

Back from the marsh-lands, or "salt-meadows,"
there was presented to our view a wide cham-
paign country, not unlike the rolling prairies of
the west. Directly in front of the station is
the site of the church where the Acadian peasants were confined. There remain to mark the
spot a row of ancient willow trees and a small
well, which latter was unearthed by the plow
only a few years since. This "well on the slope
of the hill," was accepted of course as the veritable
one that had contained "the moss grown bucket
fastened with iron, near which was a trough for
horses."

However, a regard for the truth compels us
to add that the well in question is not "on the
slope of the hill," but in the flat land near the
willows which mark the site of the church.

The Acadian peasants who settled here were
mostly emigrants from the west coast of France

and had been accustomed in their own country
to reclaim the marsh lands by building dikes to
shut out the tides. This system they pursued
here as their fathers at home in La Vandee, in
the olden time, had done before them.

It is well known that the tides rise higher
in the Bay of Minas, at the head of the Bay of
Fundy, than elsewhere on earth. At the full
of the moon, about the time of the equinoxes,
the spring tides rush up these narrow inlets
—a wall of water sixty feet high;—advancing
with a roar, the mighty waves overspread the
lowlands and crash against the dikes.

The poet refers to these immense dikes, "which
were raised by the hands of the Acadian farmers with labors incessant."

We lingered long by the site of the church
and plucked a few wild flowers by the side of
the well, to carry with us as mementoes of our
visit.

Then we turned to the north, where the prom-
ontory of Blomidon, four hundred feet high,
stands at the entrance to the Basin of Minas.

Between this headland and the site of the old
church lay the village of Grand Pré at the mouth
of the Gaspereau river. It is more appropriate,
perhaps, to term it a hamlet, as the place consists of about twenty houses scattered over the
farm-lands with not more than three or four
clustered together at the cross-roads.

All the old French houses, with their "thatched roofs, dormer windows and projecting gables," have long disappeared, and only the dikes, the willows and one apple tree remain, the work of Acadian hands. We walked along the road from the site of the old church to the mouth of the Gaspereau river, a mile distant. It was along this road, on the 10th of September, 1755, that four hundred and eighteen Acadian peasants, men and boys, were marched to the British ships that lay in the mouth of the river. They were followed to the beach by their wives and daughters bewailing their sad fate, where, as so touchingly recounted in the poem, all were forced into the ships and sent into exile, never to return.

My companion and myself stood for a time on the rude pier at the mouth of the Gaspereau, and looked down on the vessels—several schooners and a bark—that rode at anchor in the bay. Our conversation was of that time, one hundred and thirty-six years before, when from this pier, the Acadians had been crowded into the ships that then lay in this harbor. My companion said: "No doubt Evangeline had walked out on this pier, while gazing with wistful eyes for a glimpse of Gabriel." Then we spoke of the relentless cruelty practiced in the parting of families and the separation of parent from child, husband from wife, brother from sister, and alas! Evangeline from Gabriel.

But as the character of Evangeline is only a fair vision of the poet's brain, typical of some French peasant girl who dwelt here then—it is probable that but for this crucial wrong there would have been no grounds for the pathetic story, and the poet's imagery would not have cast its spell upon these fields.

The noon-hour arrived, we left the spot where the Acadians had embarked on their long exile, and walked up the hill to a cottage where we were informed we could procure accommodations. On the way we actually met the "wains" coming from the meadows, as described by the poet, "laden with the briny hay that filled the air with its odor."

This cottage was the home of a retired sea captain, a stalwart man seventy-five years of age. In the afternoon the old captain drove us all over the neighborhood, and finally back to the railroad station at Wolfville, where is situated the Acadia college. He knew all the points referred to in the poem of Evangeline, but it was his belief that the Acadians had received nothing more than their just deserts.

He was a native of this place, and we questioned him in regard to his life here, but as he had been at sea from early youth, only visiting his home at long intervals, he could tell us but little that had transpired in the meanwhile. He knew the place had changed greatly since his

childhood, and he had been told that ten or a
dozen years before there had been a large number of visitors coming every summer to Grand
Pré, but for some cause unknown to him they
had been dropping off, until now there were very
few.

While the captain was talking, we noticed his
dialect was entirely different from that of the
people among whom we had been travelling—
the French of the lower St. Lawrence, and the
English and Scotch of New Brunswick and
Prince Edward's Island.

This circumstance we mentioned to him, and
told him he talked very much like our Virginia
people. He replied that we were all of the same
stock; that he and nearly all the people about
here were descendants of the Tories who were
driven out of the United States at the close of
the Revolution, about the year 1783. They were
all exiles as well as the Acadians, and had received about as hard measure, but he had never
been told that any one had written poetry about
them! He had never known any French
people on this shore, they had all gone long before his time. He had been in command of
vessels, he said, for about thirty years, and
twice in his life he had navigated to the eastward and returned by the west, having sailed
his ship entirely around the globe.

At the captain's house we met a young man,

a native of the Bermuda Islands, who had been visiting here for several weeks. He was much interested in this place, because as he stated, "it was the scene of the events described in Evangeline," which he had read in his island home. However, it was not for that he had come here, but in search of health. He had been advised that the atmosphere of this coast would be of benefit to him, although in his islands they had spring all the time, and the fields and trees were always green. There are as many islands in the Bermudas as days in the year, but only about five of them are large enough to turn around on.

As we stood on an eminence commanding a wide prospect, he gazed with delighted eye across the grand meadows to the lofty range of the Cobequid Hills and remarked : "The world seems very large to me here in Nova Scotia, as this is the only part of the mainland I have ever been on. I am a farmer, when at home, but perhaps you would not call me a farmer but a gardener, as I have seen gardens here in Nova Scotia much larger than my farm in Bermuda. O yes, I have heard of Grand Pré many times when at home, and I regret that Mr. Longfellow could not have lived to write more good poetry."

He spoke in a lisping drawl, clipping his words after a manner peculiar to these islanders ; yet he was withal of very pleasing address. He very kindly accompanied us in our drives the whole afternoon, in order to assist the captain in pointing out the places of interest.

This is a charming valley, cultivated throughout its whole extent like a garden. Travelers say that only the valley of Wyoming in our country can match the valley of the Grand Pré in tradition and beauty; one has its Gertrude, the other its Evangeline.

We learned of a peculiar custom the farmers on this coast have of harvesting the "sedge" grass that grows on the marsh lands outside the embankments. They float their boats over the meadows, and at the ebb rest them on the grass. Without delay they now begin to cut the grass and fill their boats as rapidly as possible; then on the flood-tide they float with their cargoes of sedge-grass to the docks far inland. When they have no boats, they often employ means more hazardous. Then they go on the marshes as soon as the tide has ebbed, and cut as large bundles of grass as possible. At the turn of the tide they secure the grass with long ropes, to which is tied, at intervals, wisps of straw, in order to float it; as the tide comes up they move inshore, pulling their bundles after them. Sometimes adverse winds cause them to move slowly, and the tide gains on them at such rate that they are compelled to abandon their crops, and seek safety by fleeing to the shore.

These dike lands are, perhaps, as durable and productive as any in the world. For more than one hundred and fifty years the best of them have produced, without intermission, from two to three tons of timothy hay per acre, annually. These fertile spots well deserve the name of "the fat of the land," by which they are known to the natives.

It is sad to reflect that of the race that built these immense dikes and reclaimed this land from the hungry maw of the sea, there are now none here to enjoy its fruits. "Blown by a blast of fate like a dead leaf over the desert," they were scattered, and the soft accents of the French tongue are heard in Acadia no more.

While walking along this shore one thinks of the personages of the poem, who were identified with these scenes; of Bellefontaine and the gentle Evangeline; of sturdy Basil La Jeunesse and Gabriel; of LeBlanc and Father Felician; and there arises in memory the pitiful appeal of Evangeline when, with hope deferred, she had reached the home of her lover in far Louisiana— "Gone? is Gabriel gone?"

In the course of nature the Acadians would have passed away, but without persecution they would have left descendants behind them; now there are none of the Norman name on the coast.

Among the hardy guides and voyagers whom Fremont collected for his first Rocky Mountain expedition, there was one, by name, Basil La Jeunesse. This man, the favorite of his leader, assumed as his role always the foremost place in every danger, and finally lost his life in a perilous venture. Perhaps this circumstance may have suggested to the poet the name of the blacksmith of Grand Pré.

Mr. Longfellow never visited the scene of his poem. It is said he feared his high ideal might receive a shock from the reality; yet could he have stood with us there on that July day in the midst of the harvest, he would have perceived with the poet's eye, the landscape in all accord with his own imagery: "Peace seemed to reign on earth and the restless heart of the ocean. And pleasantly gleamed in the soft, sweet air, the Basin of Minas, as the sunset threw the long shadows of the trees o'er the broad ambrosial meads."

In all her journeyings in search of Gabriel, the poet has followed the Acadian maiden through many a sunny land—along the shores of the "Beautiful River"—over the bright prairies, "where bloom roses and purple amorphas"— across the lakes of Plaquemine, and southern Atchafalaya, where, "resplendent in beauty, the lotus lifts her golden crown"—yet in all her wanderings, Evangeline's sad gaze rested on no scene more beautiful than this view at Grand Pré—the home of her youth.

Dr. Johnson has said: "A man's patriotism should gain force upon the plain of Marathon;" likewise, the traveler in Acadia should gain in appreciation of the poem of Evangeline, on viewing the scene of the most beautiful and pathetic story in American literature.

FICTION.

PART III.

ROSE TREVILLIAN.

Mount Pinnickinnick looks loftily down,
On the valley, and on the town;
Where 'mid scenes of calm repose,
Dwells the charming,demure Rose!

The sun is just gilding the tops of the tall
hills, and the dew is on leaf and lawn, as a
girl crosses the portico of a mansion on the hillside, and trips down the steps to the walk that
winds among the trees to the park gate.

The surroundings of this residence are indic-
ative of wealth and taste, yet the elegant figure
of the girl seems to enhance the air of refinement
of the place. She passes through the gate, and
follows the road round the hill till opposite a
neat cottage where she turns aside and bows her
head beneath the low trellis of morning glories
and honeysuckles that cover the doorway.

Seated within the little room of the cottage is
an elderly lady whose refined, pale face lights
up at the sight of the girl approaching through
the bower of flowers. As she enters and places
a covered dish on the table, the old lady ex-

claims: "Why Rose, you look as pretty as the morning!"

At this the young girl stands erect; the color mounts in her pink cheeks and for an instant the silken lashes droop over her hazel eyes; then with a little laugh that falls pleasantly on the ear, she runs to the old lady—pats her on either cheek, and kisses her—after which the unexpected happens, for then she throws herself on a seat and weeps silently.

Man may explain, at times, curious phenomena of nature; but the varying moods of young women are to him inexplicable: and that this charming young person should pass suddenly from the sunshine of laughter to the storm of grief, seems alarming.

Yet the elderly lady was not much disturbed by it, but soothed the girl gently, and when a smile shone on her fair face, said: "I am surprised at you, Rose Trevillian! Here you are, crying because you have two beaux, and there's many a girl hereabouts cries because she has none at all!"

"O Aunt Annette," cried the girl, "no young lady ever had two such beaux, in the world, before. There's Lawyer Fuljames, old enough to be my father, and vain enough to be a peacock! And there's poor Tom Hilton, wild enough and nonsensical enough to be in a nursery; though he's not a day less than twenty-three! Whatever I'm to do with them, I don't know." .

And then Rose began to laugh in her very attractive way, and the old lady laughed too.

Now, while Rose and Aunt Annette are exchanging confidences, we shall take occasion to recount somewhat of her life's history.

She is an orphan; her father had died about ten years before the opening of this veracious narrative, when she was about eleven years of age. When Rose was an infant of four years she had lost her mother, and the little girl wondered often whether the dim memory of her mother's sad face that came to her on lonely nights was a reality, or the vision of a dream.

After the death of her father she had been adopted by her uncle, Colonel Ellingham, whose handsome residence we have seen her leave on this beautiful spring morning. In Colonel Effingham she had ever found a father and a protector. He was a widower and childless.

Mrs. Annette Savoy. whom Rose called "Aunt," had been his housekeeper during the tender years of her infancy; but now, for nearly two years past, Rose herself had been the mistress of his palatial residence.

Rose Trevillian had received every advantage that wealth and culture could command. After having graduated at Vassar College she was sent abroad with "Aunt Annette" as chaperon, and then for a year she had studied in the museums of Paris, and later, attended the School of Design for young ladies under the direction of the famous Rosa Bonheur. Thence, going to Berlin, she passed another year devoted to science under the private instruction of professors of the renowned University in the Linden.

At the end of this time, she found herself well versed in three languages. Her mind had been broadened by observation and travel; her active intellect, stimulated by her intercourse with brilliant people of two continents.

Yet, when Rose returned to her native land, she found things sadly changed at home; her uncle's usually cheerful countenance now bore a careworn expression: he seemed ill at ease, until he had informed his niece of the changed condition of his affairs, which would necessitate a great change in their manner of life.

"I have become very much embarrassed financially, my child," he said, "and we may expect, sooner or later, to be sold out of house and home." However, they had continued to struggle along for nearly two years since the return of Rose, living in their beautiful home, pretty much after the old style. It is true that Rose had taught a class in fine arts during this period, and thus contributed her moiety to the household expenses.

In fact the old colonel's embarrassment was perhaps more in anticipation than in reality.

Meanwhile, Miss Rose had written a novel which

had been published only eighteen months, and had begun already to yield considerable revenue.

The success of Rose's adventure in literature was a surprise to her friends, not because they thought her incapable of writing a novel, but because she persisted in choosing for her subject one so incongruous with the life and thoughts of a young lady; one, they said, she could not possibly know much about. For, despite their objections, it had pleased her to write a tale of the sea, entitled: "The Captain of the Bellerophon; A Tale of Nantucket."

Now to find out what a young lady could possibly know about seafaring, even one as gifted as Rose, was the curiosity that had prompted many young men and a few mariners to read the novel written by "Rose Trevillian."

For she persisted also in writing under her own proper name; but this was not an objection offered by the gentlemen of her acquaintance; for they declared that no *nom-de-plume* she could have assumed would have sounded so well to them.

Those who read her book were warm in their praises of it and one or two professional critics wrote of it, in such terms that her friends said: "Rose is about to wake up some morning and find herself famous." One critic wrote: "She has written a graphic story of the sea; her knowledge of nautical terms is surprising, and her sea-tale is natural, lifelike and of absorbing interest. We predict it will be read by mariners wherever the English language is known."

The subject of Rose Trevillian's novel had been suggested to her mind by a tragic incident that had occurred on her voyage to Europe, which may be briefly stated.

As her steamer crossed the Grand Banks the "look out" had sighted the wreck of what proved to be a Nantucket fishing smack which had been crushed by contact with an iceberg. From a bit of this wreck Rose had seen the sailors snatch the dank, limp form of the captain of the ill-fated craft, the only survivor of a crew of thirteen. She was standing near the rail of her ship when his almost lifeless body was lifted on board; and her woman's heart was touched with pity as she noted that his bronzed face, though tinged with the pallor of death, still wore an expression of resolution and that his hand still grasped the trumpet, while those who had answered its call were beneath the waves.

After a time the surgeons succeeded in bringing this man back to life and a week later, when he was serving in the capacity of a boatswain on her ship, Rose had noticed him, as he was standing forward directing the sailors aloft, through the same battered trumpet he had brought from the wreck, she felt drawn to speak to him. So after his task was finished she called him aside to the cabin door and "questioned him the story of his life."

He replied in frank and sailor-like phrase that added a picturesque effect to his narrative of perils and sufferings on the sea.

This incident made such an impression on her youthful mind that it did not fade from her memory, and when two years later she began her novel it must needs be a story of the sea, and the Nantucket captain must of course be the chief hero of her narrative.

This is the explanation that Rose gave to her friends in regard to the origin of her story that is now so much read by "those that go down to the sea in ships, that do business in great waters."

Now that Rose has just ended her conversation with "Aunt Annette" and is leaving the cottage, we shall go with her.

It is a remarkable coincidence that as soon as she reaches the pavement a young man should drive up to the sidewalk with his buggy. He pretends to be much surprised to meet her; however, he jumps out, doffs his hat, and begs the honor of driving her home.

Rose consents with a pretty air and Mr. Tom Hilton, for 'tis he, assists her to a seat in his vehicle which, by the way, is rather a ramshackle affair, although the horse is a good one.

Tom Hilton is a tall man of florid complexion

with a sandy moustache and a smiling, pleasant countenance. He is the son of a wealthy farmer living in the suburbs of the town.

"The shortest way home is the longest way around," remarked Tom as they started. Now, although he misquoted the proverb and perhaps did not care for its significance, yet he interpreted it very handsomely, that is to suit himself, and made considerable of a detour from the direct route.

But as they turned toward home and after Tom had talked himself to a standstill on matters personal, he thought it best to change the subject and try to be really entertaining. So he said: "Miss Rose, the thermometer had a late fall this spring!" At this his companion broke down completely and began to laugh.

Thereupon, he began to jest with her about her novel, and he wanted to know, "whether the captain's gig was drawn by a sea horse!" Continuing, he stated very gravely that "her sea-story was so natural the publishers said they could see its sails!"

They were nearly opposite the court house by this time and Tom was about to "get off" something else, when there was a crackling noise heard somewhere about the old buggy. Tom pulled up his horse and Rose hopped lightly out; but as he was about to follow one of the hind wheels crashed down and he rolled over backwards and fell out!

Tom scrambled to his feet and was clawing the mud from his coat when he observed his rival, Lawyer Fuljames, advancing, hat in hand, and bowing most obsequiously to Miss Rose. Mr. Fuljames proposed very politely to relieve Mr. Hilton of his present embarrassment by escorting Miss Trevillian home.

It was the only thing to be done, as Hilton could not leave the horse, so he had to be content with the sweet words of sympathy that fell from Rose's lips in regard to the accident, and then to see her depart, walking up the hill with the man of all others he feared most as a rival. It seemed to him that Fuljames had some secret hold or unknown influence over Col. Effingham, the uncle of Rose, and through him he appeared to exercise some influence over her out of all proportion to his deserts when one considers the age of the lawyer and his personal appearance.

"What was there about this man to attract any young lady?" that was the question Hilton had asked himself on many occasions and could not answer.

Lawyer Augustus Fuljames was about fifty years or age, of medium stature and rotund figure, with small twinkling eyes; his sandy goatee was died black in spots; his dress was of the shabby genteel style and there was that about the man to excite in a stranger a feeling of distrust. In fact there was a general air of insincerity and a want of conviction in what he said, as if he were always shifting and tacking to avoid controversy or the giving of offense. He was a lawyer of great shrewdness, and many said, unscrupulous and heartless in his dealings; and as a sequence was successful and had acquired a large fortune.

As the lawyer and Miss Rose walked up the hill together he began to harp on the subject that had of late distressed her much; but now that he was much more importunate and much bolder than ever, she was driven to answer him with firmness, that he need never approach her on the subject of matrimony as it was an endeavor hopeless on his part and one that always gave her pain.

Fuljames then, flushed with anger and disappointment, spoke to her insolently and as a craven.

"I have been very patient with your foster father, Col. Effingham," he said. "But now I shall push matters as becomes a man of business. I don't think it is at all necessary for you to put on so many airs with me, when I own the very house over your head, and your foster-father has remained there only through my charity and at my expense!"

By this time they were near the entrance to Col. Effingham's fine grounds, and at this unmanly speech of Fuljames, Rose turned on him with flashing eyes: "Go," she exclaimed "and never speak to me again, sir!"

The man slunk from her presence with a dejected air but went away shaking his head and mumbling threats.

II.

Rose Trevillian's indignation aroused by the insolent language of Lawyer Fuljames caused her to walk with a very stately step through the winding way of the park, while she resolved in her mind what part of this conversation should be divulged to her uncle.

She knew his impetuous temper and feared the consequences that might ensue; yet she considered it a duty to inform him of the lawyer's threats so that if he could provide any stay for the threatened legal process he would have time to act.

As Rose approached the house, Col. Effingham, a tall white-haired man of very imposing presence, was walking back and forth on the portico. He noticed at once the agitation of his niece, and as she walked by his side and recounted to him her conversation with the lawyer, the old colonel began to bring his cane down with great force, and then to saw the air with it as if he held a saber in his hand and was making "cuts and thrusts."

His language was very emphatic and decisive

in regard to the character and conduct of Fuljames, and it took all of Rose's persuasive powers to make him promise that he would not
"wear his cane out on that 'pettifogger,' on
sight!"

He admitted, finally, that "it would be dis-
graceful for a man like himself who had led soldiers in battle to have a personal encounter with
an ignoble foeman like Fuljames."

Col. Ellingham was a gray-haired man, even
in time of the war with Mexico, now ten years
past; for one of his officers then wrote home:
"Our 'Plume of Navarre' is our colonel's white
head, for it shines through the smoke, and we
have to spur very hard to keep up with the 'old
man,' so he won't do all the charging by himself!"

Hence, it is easy to be seen, the colonel is now
too old a man to begin life anew should his property be taken from him, which seemed probable.
He had been induced to go on the notes of a
brother officer, Colonel Dalton, who owned large
possessions in the shape of valuable pine forests
in North Carolina.

Colonel Dalton died the year after the Mexican War, and Ellingham claimed that the principal note had been paid, as his friend had
written to him to that effect; but through some
mischance this note had not been canceled, but
had fallen into the hands of Lawyer Fuljames

for collection. Now, as it happened, Effingham was the only responsible endorser left, and the note with the interest added amounted to a great sum, more than his estate would pay. Such was the present condition of his affairs.

Colonel Dalton had left a son, Edward, who had been a captain of cavalry under Effingham, and was a great favorite with him. In fact, it was largely due to his great affection for this gallant Captain Edward Dalton, that had chiefly influenced Colonel Effingham to assist his father, to the extent of greatly embarrassing himself.

The year his father had died, Edward Dalton had gone to sea as the captain of a merchant ship, and had now been absent from the country for ten years. Colonel Effingham had tried in vain to communicate with him.

He believed that Edward Dalton knew this debt had been paid before he left the country, otherwise, he would not have departed, and left his old colonel in the lurch to pay a debt of which he had not received one dollar.

"My only hope," said the colonel, "is to delay legal process in this business until Edward Dalton shall return to settle with the administrator's of his father's estate. This is the hope that has long sustained me, but now, that Fuljames is smarting under his rebuff—I fear he will push matters to extremity."

The gentle Rose was very sorrowful as she

looked in her uncle's careworn face and felt as though she were to blame for increasing the anxieties that were weighing him down.

Before she left him and passed into the house, she said: "O Uncle, I am so sorry, so very sorry; yet what could I do?"

Rose had uttered these modest words in low, sweet tones; for she possessed that characteristic token of refinement—"a voice ever soft, gentle and low."

Yet the old soldier would not let her make an apology in extenuation of her rebuff of Fuljames, but said, as he laid his hand on her head:

"My child, you did exactly right; you must never think of this man any more. The gyrfalcon does not mate with the carrion crow! I knew your father well, and rode by his side in battle; he was a brave and honorable man; and were he alive to-day, he would have it so." The old man kissed her and she tried to smile, but tears were in her eyes as she passed on into the house with a sad heart.

Coincident with these occurrences the spring term of the "Federal Court" was holding in the town, and there were many visiting lawyers and strangers in attendance. In honor of these visitors the citizens were to give a large ball that night at the "Old Stone Tavern." But more especially did the towns-people wish to honor the able and dignified court—a judge profoundly versed in legal knowledge and yet endowed with such courtly and affable manners as rendered him everywhere a great favorite in society.

Soon after the shades of night had fallen the old tavern was ablaze with candle light, and here the eager and expectant élite of the town were assembled.

To Lawyer Fuljames had been assigned the pleasing task of escorting Miss Rose Trevillian to the ball. But after the *contretemps* of the morning, of course, this could not be.

The ceremonies were about to begin; the strains of music were heard; and the jocund laugh, and all the merriment that precedes the giddy whirl of the dance, were on; when on looking around for their partners, the young men noticed that one of the fairest of the fair was missing!

Tom Hilton exclaimed with a tragic air: "The sun has gone down at noon-day! I no longer take any interest in life!"

But when young Cameron, one of the exquisites of the town, sidled up to him and whispered: "Tom there's old Fuljames over there, fuller than a biled owl! Miss Rose wouldn't come with him in that condition—of course not!"

Then Hilton, despite his words, began to take considerable "interest in life;" for he gazed at Fuljames for a moment, and there was a dangerous glint in his eyes as he noted the disreputable plight of the lawyer. But he said nothing about it, but merely remarked to young Cameron, as he turned aside: "I depart immediately, in quest of the queen of the ball," and left the house.

Tom Hilton arrived at the residence of Col. Effingham soon after Miss Rose, arrayed in a Worth costume, had taken her seat in the parlor to await her uncle, who, she supposed, would escort her to the grand ball which had been looked forward to as the event of the season.

Tom was ushered into the parlor without being aware of her presence, and his eyes falling on her, as she sat silent and motionless, she appeared to him a vision of loveliness beyond compare.

Indeed his surprise, shown by his silence and awkward attitude, appeared so ludicrous that Miss Rose exclaimed, laughing:

"Why, Tom, you didn't take me for a ghost, did you?"

"For a ghost," drawled Tom. "I took you for an angel, fresh from the shores of the blest!"

It was now Miss Rose's turn to be abashed at this warmth of expression which bore the unmistakable ring of true feeling, and she hung her head and colored very prettily, as she said:

"O Tom, you are too ridiculous for anything!"

Now this was rather a weak remark to fall from the lips of the dignified and learned Miss

Rose Trevillian, and really showed how much she was embarrassed by the unbridled admiration of her suitor.

III.

Tom Hilton had not much time to reflect upon the criticism made by Miss Rose Trevillian, that his remark was—"too ridiculous for anything."

For Col. Effingham appeared at the parlor door soon thereafter and directed them to go on without awaiting him. "Tell the judge," he said, "I'll be along pretty soon and give him such a rubber at whist as will remind him of old days. Nothing will please the old man more than that," he concluded; "for he dearly loves a rubber at whist."

These orders Tom essayed very cheerfully to carry out, but as they went along he seemed possessed for the nonce with a desire to talk about Lawyer Fuljames. Miss Rose changed the subject very adroitly several times, but Mr. Hilton still persisted in turning the conversation to that noted lawyer, till Miss Rose finally said: "Tom, please never mention Mr. Fuljames' name to me again; I ask this of you as a favor!"

"There's nobody on earth I'd sooner quit talking about than Fuljames!" exclaimed Tom. "For my part, Miss Rose," he continued, "I wish one of those sea-porpoises you wrote about in your book would swallow him!

"I don't know whether a porpoise could swallow a man, but I don't think it would take a very big fish to swallow a small potato like Fuljames!"

But as these vagaries evoked no reply from his companion, the forbidden name was not again mentioned.

Mr. Hilton arrived at the ball-room in time to sail through the first cotillion, and also through the first waltz with his charming companion; after which, finding that he could not retain possession much longer—he escorted her the length of the room, that they might pay their respects to the distinguished judge, who had requested the pleasure of again meeting Miss Rose.

The courtly judge took her by both hands, as he spoke to her of her gallant father, whom he had known; and then he complimented her on her book which "he had read, not only with interest, but with profit. I have informed my law class that your book is, in my opinion, a work of genius; and now I take this occasion to thank you for your contribution to literature. Yes, my young lady, for such a story as brings gladness to eyes that fail with wakefulness, and consoles sorrow, this, I conceive, is the noblest form of fiction."

Rose was very happy at commendation of her writing coming from such high authority, and there were no clouds to mar the festivities of the evening; but all went "merry as marriage bells," till the late hour when the tired dancers sought repose.

However, there was a little episode "after the ball," not down on the programme.

As Mr. Tom Hilton was walking past the hotel "after seeing Miss Rose home," he was accosted by Lawyer Fuljames, who with others stood in front of the billiard room, the window of which was still open, although it was then in the small hours of the morning.

Fuljames called out in a blatant tone: "Hello! Hilton, if you are after money, you'd better let Miss Rose alone, and go for Miss Silverside!"

Hilton turned, and said fiercely: "I'll go for you, you—" just then Fuljames aimed a blow with his cane at Tom's head, which he warded off with his left arm; and before he could repeat it, Tom straightened out his strong right arm— his fist striking Fuljames squarely on the mouth, and actually driving him through the window into the billiard room. There he lay for a time motionless, with his feet protruding from the sill, the only part of his body in view from the street!

There was a great commotion about the tavern; the landlord, a friend of Fuljames, ran out and caught Tom roughly by the shoulder; but by this time Hilton's mettle was well up and the

landlord went down instantly before his powerful stroke. Then looking around very fiercely,
Hilton said: "I've a notion to go in there and
finish that one-horse lawyer!"

But some of the young men gathered about
him and persuaded him not to do it, and as his
arm pained him severely he concluded to go down
to the office of Dr. Squills and have it dressed.

When Tom appeared at the office of Dr. Squills
that gentleman was about to retire after the
fatigues of the ball.

He examined the wounded arm with a very critical eye and pronounced: "No fracture, but if
there had been one it would have been a compound
or a comminuted complex one!"

However, he fixed it up with bandages and
opodeldoc so that it was very comfortable.

Then Hilton called out: "Doe," said he, "how
will a little *spiritus frumenti* set on me after the
exercises of the evening?"

But the learned physician declared "it would
increase the fever of his wound," and that "he
must forego that indulgence for the present."

The doctor who had gotten an inkling of the
brawl was curious to know "whether the landlord or Fuljames had received any fractures or
mortal wounds?"

"I don't know," replied Tom to this query,
"I only know that the landlord went down, and
that I knocked Fuljames out of sight!"

On the next day the doctor laughed heartily as he came to understand the significance of Tom's reply as it had reference to Fuljames.

Now let us turn from the trivial incidents of this brawl and take up one of the scattered strands that must be woven into the fabric of this true tale; "for aught that we could ever read, could ever hear by tale or history, the course of true love never did run smooth."

If we could trace to their source the diverse influences that cross like threads in the warp of life and shape our destiny, we should be led into distant scenes and among strange fellowships beyond the power of imagination to conceive.

Even now after the grand ball at the "Stone Tavern," if we shall take the wings of a dove and fly far to the eastward; far beyond the first ocean and the night, and then far beyond the second ocean till the day wanes toward the second night, we shall then be in that distant tropical sea where spice islands gem the waves and "the amber scent of odorous perfumes" fills the air, and where fronded palms spread their foliage to the torrid sun.

Here we shall see a stately ship, foreign from beak to taffrail, sailing majestically over the silent waters.

We go aboard this foreign frigate where no sound of English speech is heard. All the crew are "Lascars," the officers too are of the Malay race; but surely the captain, who now gives over the watch to the first officer and walks aft, is not of this race. For as he lifts his cap from his swarthy face and smoothes back his dark locks, he displays a brow too fair for that of a Lascar.

He enters his cabin and we shall enter with him, for this man is none other than Edward Dalton, the captain of the ship and the former comrade-in-arms of Col. Ellingham.

Now it is the custom of Captain Dalton, when alone, to talk aloud to himself in the English language that he may not forget his native speech during his long exile from his country.

On entering the cabin he approaches a small desk containing books which he examines, saying: "I'll see what Raoul gave me to read at Manila. I ordered him to give me English works"— then he lapses into the languages of the books— talks for quite a while—recovers himself and repeats in English—"I am tired of Dutch and Spanish and the Lascar lingo—no, here is one— 'The Captain of the Bellerophon: A Tale of Nantucket,' by 'Rose Trevillian.'

"Well, well, I'll have to read it for the sake of the English." And then he prepares his easy chair, turning it to the light of the port, also arranges his lamp to have it ready as the evening draws on apace.

"What does a woman know about a sea captain?" he says, scanning the title curiously as he takes up the novel.

"Trevillian? where have I known that name—oh, yes—the colonel of the cavalry—the friend of my old colonel—Effingham! What a flood of memories these names revive. I've been a wanderer for a long time and have led an eventful life; now I am thirty-two and with a competency earned I shall soon return to my native hills and renew the friendships of my youth."

And then Captain Dalton begins to read, and he reads on, and the stars come up and go down and still he reads on; and when he turns the last leaf and "turns in" the day is dawning on the Banda Sea.

Now when next we shall meet this ship-captain of the Indies, it may, peradventure, be in the town where we left the tired dancers asleep.

IV.

Whatever the future may have in store of good or evil fortune, it is a true saying: "The veil which covers the face of futurity is woven by the hand of mercy."

Winter has returned and a deep snow lies on the ground when we again see Miss Rose Trevillian walking down into the town from her uncle's residence on the hill.

The scene is as different from a former one as

the season is different; for now she is well muf-
fled in furs, and trips along through the snow
at a lively step to keep warm. As she approaches
the crossing to the principal street, she notices
Lawyer Fuljames in conversation with a very
distinguished looking stranger.

This man's face was turned from her, but his
air and figure presented such a strikingly favorable contrast to that of Fuljames that almost
any young lady would have noticed him.

Rose passed within a few feet of them and
had already reached the middle of the street
when there came to her ears a sound as of the
breath of the North wind—sonorous, and commanding in intonation as if from the blast of a
trumpet—"Avast! there, Lassie! the craft will
run ye down!"

Rose turned and was horrified to see a runaway horse, with the wreck of a sleigh flying at
his heels, almost upon her!

He carried no bells, and she had not heard
the thud of his hoofs in the snow.

She hesitated; what was she to do—run back,
or run forward?

In that supreme moment a strong arm clasped
her waist; she was lifted from the ground and
in a bound or two the tall stranger stood on the
pavement, holding Rose under his arm as he
would a sack of salt.

The man was still looking after the horse

which a short distance beyond fell—striking his
head against a tree—and stretched himself in
death.

Meanwhile Miss Rose was struggling, and even
kicking, in an undignified way to rid herself
from the clasp of her rescuer.

The stranger, when he turned his head and
looked at her, set her down instantly and appeared much embarrassed. He even took off his
hat, and tried to apologize to her; but Rose, being confused, did not know what he was saying.

But her own thoughts were—"What a sun-
browned, handsome face! Pity that scar; maybe
he's a soldier—but his speech is that of a sailor.
'Avast! there, lassie!' That's the way he hails
me! He saved my life, I ought to thank him."

Miss Rose remembered afterwards with morti-
fication, that she did not speak one word to
the stranger.

However, "she shook herself, and primped
her feathers like a wet duck." At least that's
what Miss Silverside said, and she lives opposite the place of the accident, and "saw it all."

That young lady ran across the street, and
took the very much agitated Miss Rose into her
own house, and ministered to her wants—chat-
tering all the time.

The stranger walked away down the street,
and disappeared. "Rose, you did struggle
mightily, and kicked too," laughed Miss Silver-

side. "And he was such a handsome man,"
she cried. "But you are not used to being run
over, or hugged either, Rose, and you were mor-
tally skeered, no doubt."

"He didn't even look at me," replied Rose,
"until he had seen what had become of the horse.
He certainly is handsome; he saved my life, but
he has a grip like a grizzly bear: my ribs ache
yet."

Miss Rose Trevillian had been invited to spend
the day with one of her friends; she was on her
way to that friend's house when she met with
the thrilling adventure that may change the current of her whole life.

After she had become somewhat composed,
she left Miss Silverside and repaired to her
friend's house. Here she recounted, in her modest, fascinating way, her mishaps of the morning. A thousand surmises were made by the
young ladies present in regard to the "gallant
stranger;" but their curiosity was not to be grat-
ified on that day.

The next morning when Miss Rose met her
uncle, Col. Effingham, at the breakfast table,
she was surprised to find him in such excellent
spirits; in fact he appeared almost ten years
younger than on the day before.

He approached her with a glad smile, and taking her by both hands, said: "My lassie, our
troubles are all over."

Now Rose's first thought was, "Whoever called me 'Lassie' before? Oh, that whirlwind of a stranger when he snatched me from the earth! But what could her uncle mean?"

While they were at the table, Col. Effingham explained to his niece that on the day before, when she was absent, he had received a visit from Captain Dalton, his former comrade-in-arms, whom he had not met for many years.

Captain Dalton had come all the way from the sea-port in order to pay his respects to his old colonel, and to apologize to him for the great trouble that he, Effingham, had involved himself in, indorsing notes for his father.

"But now he has removed all these troubles," the colonel said, "for he has settled all claims against his father's estate. He informed me also, that he gave Lawyer Fuljames 'a round rating' in regard to the rascally manner in which he had managed the business.

"I am now very happy for I don't owe a cent in the world but am rich again," he said. "I am also well pleased that I have not been deceived in Captain Dalton; but I never doubted him for a moment. I have invited him to dine with us to-morrow, Rose, when I shall take great pleasure in presenting you to one of the most gallant men I have ever known!"

"What is the personal appearance of Captain Dalton?" inquired the demure Rose. She was all anxiety, for she began to suspect that he and the handsome stranger who had delivered her safe from the hoofs of the runaway horse were one and the same.

"Oh, well, child," replied the colonel, "he's good enough for looks, in fact, he's a very handsome man; but he's better far than he looks: he's as true as steel! you shall see him tomorrow."

Rose then recounted to her uncle her fearful escape from death—how the stranger, at great peril to himself, had snatched her from under the horse's feet. She then described her rescuer minutely, his manner and dress. Before she had finished, the colonel exclaimed:

"Of course that's Dalton!—just like him not to say anything about it."

Miss Rose was somewhat disturbed that Captain Dalton had not thought worthy of mention the thrilling adventure in which he had saved her life. Yet she consoled herself with the reflection that he did not know her and of course was not aware that this adventure could be a matter of interest to Colonel Effingham.

She was very busy all that day in preparing for the dinner party to be given on the morrow to this Captain Dalton of whom her uncle had spoken in terms of such ardent friendship. She appeared unusually bright and happy; there was a warm flush on her cheeks and her beautiful eyes shone with a glad light which her friends had not noted before.

Col. Effingham had invited a few old army officers of the neighborhood to meet Dalton; Miss Rose also invited some of her young friends, among whom were Miss Editha Silverside and Mr. Tom Hilton.

It was soon noised abroad in the town that Miss Rose Trevillian had been saved from almost certain death by a daring stranger who in his effort to rescue her from being trampled to death by a runaway horse, had greatly imperilled his own life.

Then it became the desire of many to see him, and the story of the intrepid act that had brought Captain Dalton into public notice, was very much exaggerated as it passed from one to another.

V.

O well for the sailor when on that day,
He turns from the charm of the sea away,
For the fairest flower of the beautiful hills—
For the love of Rose his true heart thrills—
And the sailor forgets the charm of the sea,
For her love does surpass the charm of the sea!

The candles were lighted in the spacious parlors of Col. Effingham's residence, and most of the guests had assembled when Captain Dalton was observed walking leisurely through the winding way of the approach.

Miss Rose thought it unfortunate that her

uncle at that moment was seated on the side portico enjoying a smoke with one of his brother officers and that she was left alone to do the honors of the occasion. It is true, "Aunt Annette" is there to assist her, but Rose thought her uncle's presence would have made the introduction less embarrassing.

"Aunt Annette" met the captain at the parlor door and led him forward to introduce him; she noticed as his eyes fell on the charming hostess that he changed color visibly beneath all the darkness of his sea-bronzed face. He evidently recognized her but went through the ceremony creditably, perhaps with the thought that he himself was not recognized.

It was only after Miss Rose in very choice and appropriate phrase had thanked him for saving her life and apologized for not having done so at the time of the accident, that the captain seemed really discomfited.

He hesitated, then said: "Please don't mention it, Miss Trevillian—a little matter like that —pray don't notice it!"

"A little matter like that!" reiterated Miss Rose, who now that she observed the captain so much disconcerted, rapidly regained confidence, and replied smartly : "Do you call it, sir, a small matter—the saving of my life?"

"Oh no, lady, I did not mean that! I meant —oh, you know what I meant"—and then they both laughed, and the ice was broken.

Captain Edward Dalton proved to be an interesting man in conversation; there were present not only his old colonel but three or four army officers who had known him in youth. He was a favorite with them all and soon became so with his new acquaintances.

There was much merriment at the table over the account of "the rescue of Rose" as narrated by Miss Editha Silverside, a society belle, and the only eye witness to the occurrence, save Lawyer Fuljames, who of course was not present at this dinner party.

Mr. Tom Hilton carried himself with a very jaunty air on this festive occasion, but his heart was not light. He remarked aside to young Cameron: "I believe this Dalton is the very sea-captain Rose wrote her book about; and now he has to come out here and rescue her!

"Why couldn't I have been there when old Bartow's horse was about to run over her! Luck never did light on me. I'm afraid my cake is all dough!"

Thus he rattled on to the amusement of several young men in the corner of the room, while Miss Rose and the gallant captain were promenading on the portico.

Later on in the evening several of the younger set of the young ladies gathered about Mr. Hilton, and began to twit him about his new rival.

Tom bore it all in good part till one of these

Job's comforters kindly suggested: "He might make away with Captain Dalton as he had done with Mr. Fuljames!"

To this Tom then made reply, very slowly and gravely: "It is so much easier to forgive a big man than a little one!"

This repartee amused the girls and they continued their thrusts at his expense, until he finally remarked: "Young ladies when a man is under a cloud, the silver lining is on the other side —that is the *silverside*!" Thereupon, with a solemn mien he walked across the room and seated himself beside Miss Editha Silverside!

This was more than the girls could stand, and they giggled outrageously; so that it required all of Mr. Hilton's ingenuity in prevarication to smoothe over matters with the prim and polished Miss Silverside.

Captain Dalton was quite the lion of the evening, especially among the ladies; but he was not a demonstrative man and bore his honors meekly.

The old officers told aside and in undertones of his deeds as a boy captain. He himself appeared much touched by the revival of old memories and the cordial reception and the kind remembrances of his comrades.

But of late years his life had been cast among a different class, and amid foreign scenes. Yet of his adventures on the seas he did not speak, and there was no one present who could do so.

He had stated on his first appearance at the inn that he would probably remain for a few days, only, until he could see some old friends and renew some old acquaintances. Yet he had remained for many days; but rumor said, more on account of new friends than old ones.

However this may be, Captain Dalton was in constant attendance upon the charming Miss Rose; in riding and driving and wandering over hill lands, he was her very shadow.

He told Col. Effingham that "his old cavalry instincts had come back to him as soon as he had put foot on land."

This was given in explanation of the fact that he had just received from Kentucky two very fine thorough-bred saddle horses.

It was a fine sight to see Miss Rose and the captain riding through the forest avenues when they were ablaze with all the autumn hues.

The captain said that never in foreign lands had he seen "Such beauty and splendor, and that it made his heart glad!"

As he looked toward the peerless horsewoman at his side, when he spake this—he doubtless spoke in all candor and sincerity!

Miss Silverside and all the other gossips of the town knew exactly how all this was to end; and they were right—at least in this instance.

It happened in this wise, but how it was found out is not known.

It was a beautiful morning in Autumn; Miss Rose and the captain were riding along a forest path, alight with the blaze of the rising sun, and the glories of the season.

Such was the situation when the captain began all at once to talk in a peculiar fashion—using sailor-terms and sea-jargon, as Miss Rose had never heard him do before.

But in a little while she became aware that he was quoting passages from her own novel.

As soon as she became conscious of this, Miss Rose colored a rosy red, which did not detract from her good looks at all, so thought the captain. But she would not stand much of this, so turning to him, she said: "Why captain! you remind me of Mr. Hilton, the way you are talking now!"

His reply was: "I think Mr. Hilton a very clever fellow."

Then Miss Rose continued: "Where on earth did you ever see my book?"

"Your book!" exclaimed the captain. "Why are you the Miss Trevillian who wrote the great sea novel? Well, well, I'll say first I read your book while sailing over the Banda Sea."

"And where is the Banda Sea?" asked Miss Rose irrelevantly, in her happy confusion not knowing very well what to say.

"Many miles from these beautiful hills," the captain replied. "Your book fell into my hands

by accident at sea. I began to read it one lonely
night, and soon became so much interested in it
that I continued to read until I finished it—
reading all night."

"You don't mean to say—you read my book
all night!" exclaimed the astonished and well
pleased Miss Rose.

"*Cela va sans dire!*" replied the captain in
his eagerness to assure her.

And then he thanked her politely for the entertainment her book had afforded him when
lonely and surrounded by those who did not
speak his native language.

'Twas then he spoke of his deep affection for
her, and the new-born hope that had arisen in
his heart; and pleaded his cause in such frank
and manly phrase that the gentle Rose could
not conceal the riotous joy that mantled in her
cheeks, and the bold captain would take no
refusal!

One evening, a few weeks later, as this couple
were promenading on the portico, they noticed
Col. Effingham regarding them with a wistful
look, as if he had that in his heart which he
refrained from speaking.

Then, after a whispered consultation, the
captain led the blushing Rose to her uncle's
side, and said: "Colonel, you once called me
your son on the battlefield; can you not do so
now that Rose has promised to be my wife!"

The old colonel seemed stricken with sudden joy; he kissed Rose, and hopped about for very gladness.

In congratulating the captain he told him he would be in honor bound to name his next ship the "Bellerophon."

The debonair Dalton bowed low in gracious courtesy to his fiancee, as he replied: "If I ever sail the seas again, my vessel shall be called the 'Bellerophon;' and her figure-head shall be adorned with a 'Rose'—the fairest flower that ever bloomed on land to charm a sailor from the sea."

One of the prettiest weddings ever seen, and remembered because of many distinguished strangers in attendance, was celebrated in the "Church under the Maples."

This took place in the glorious "Month of Roses," when the fragrance of flowers revives in memory the beautiful creations of the old poets. Then we think of Herrick's "Sappho," how the Roses were all white until they tried to rival her fair complexion, and blushing for shame because they were vanquished, have ever since remained red. And of the lovelorn Juliet as she mused on the moonlit balcony thinking that "the rose by any other name would smell as sweet."

And of old Chaucer's "Emilie" with hair blown backward gathering roses in the early morning: "thrusts among the thorns her little hand." And of Milton's "Eve" as she stands in Eden half veiled in a cloud of fragrance, "so thick the blushing roses round her blow."

The roses were also very thick at the marriage ceremony of Captain Edward Dalton and Miss Rose Trevillian; for the good ship "Bellerophon" was there *en miniature*, laden with a cargo of rarest roses!

The church was packed from altar rail to entrance with the fashionables of the town.

Well up in front, on the right, sat Miss Editha Silverside in gorgeous apparel, as prim as the erect, yellow primrose!

Well up in front, on the left, sat Mr. Tom Hilton in stunning array, still trying to keep on the *silverside* of the cloud "that lowered upon his house!" The queenly Rose, escorted by her distinguished relative, Col. Ellingham, was accompanied by two very comely bridesmaids, while on seats contiguous sat five army officers, in supporting distance of their old colonel.

The bridegroom, this gallant son of Mars and of Neptune, was also accompanied by two attendants; one of them an army officer; but his best man was a sea-captain whose brown face presented a striking contrast to the pearly complexions of the bridesmaids.

On a seat hard by were a trio of foreign mariners, like sea-gulls on a spar. They had ventured thus far from the salt water, as they said in their dialect: "To honor the captain and the winsome lassie, who wrote the great sea book!"

Of those present on this joyous occasion there remain some who will contend even to this day, that this was "the loveliest wedding" ever celebrated in the "Church under the Maples."

THE LIGHT THAT FAILED.

Many years ago, within a dimly lighted room of an old manor-house, on Chesapeake Bay, two men sat at cards. The dead silence of the night, or rather of the early morning, reigned over the place. Much money lay piled on the table; while the tensely drawn features and eager interest of the players showed the desperate nature of the game. At last, the elder man threw down his hand of cards with a great thump, as he swept the money from the board, and exclaimed:

"That's a huckleberry above your persimmon!"

"When you hold all the aces in the pack, my loss is a foregone conclusion," replied his opponent, as he turned around and rested his head on the back of his chair.

"Oh, well, Bill," said the elder man, as he gazed into the handsome, dark features of his young companion, "all you've got to do is to call on the old man when you need funds;" and he stowed his winnings into the pocket of his coat.

"Not much," said Bill, "I think I've eaten my white bread; since father's second marriage, he don't seem to show me much favor, and I've resolved to quit this house, where I have scant welcome, and again seek my fortune beyond seas."

"Why Bill, you are the only legal heir to your mother's large estate, your father has only a life interest in it, and he cannot keep you out of it."

"Well, he is doing it anyway; he has recorded the will of my mother, which conveys the property to himself, 'her beloved husband.'"

While the speaker, William Walcott, was recounting this, his hearer, Lawyer Chapman, listened with manifest interest.

After a long pause, the lawyer said: "Bill, there must be something wrong about this business; I knew your mother when she was young, and I was young, and a kinder woman never lived on the earth. She never disinherited her only child, though that child was yourself, a wild rover, in foreign parts when she died."

In this strain he talked for some time, but the young man made no reply. Finally the old lawyer, in a querulous tone, said:

"Why don't you talk? When did you first hear of this will, before your father's second marriage, or only since your new mother came on the tapis?"

Thus appealed to, the young man sat up and smoothed back his hair; but he paused in thought, before he said: "The will was recorded within the last month. I never heard of it before, but I hear much of it now; especially from my new mother; and finding myself an unwel-

come guest in my own house, I have resolved to
quit"—he stopped suddenly, arose, and relieved his feelings by kicking the chair across
the room. This raised a great noise which re-
echoed in the wainscoted room of the old mansion; when this had subsided, the lawyer whis-
tled low: "Is it so bad as that?" he said; then
he put his hand under his coat slowly, and as if
with great reluctance, drew forth the money he
had won. This he handed to the young man,
saying: "Take that, William, I never pluck a
wounded pigeon; you'll need that on your travels, for I see you are going, and I don't blame
you; however, I'll keep back a tenner for contin-
gent expenses," he said on second thought, as
he withdrew that amount. "The other you can
repay me when you are able," he concluded.
"But are you sure this will is all regular?"

"I asked Guilford, who, as you know, has
been the family lawyer for many years, to inquire into the matter. He expressed great surprise that he had not known of the will before,
but upon searching the records, he declared that
it was all regular and that I had been disinherited. He is a cautious man, and while he says
this, he will look at me and shake his head in
doubt and wonder."

Chapman's only reply was: "Guilford is a
good lawyer and he may well shake his head
over such business as this!" Then he looked at

his watch, and remarked: "It is now in the wee small hours and it is time to be going."

Walcott then walked around the table and said, as he took the old lawyer by the hand: "Mr. Chapman, I shall remember your kindness to me; it may be long, if ever, before we meet again; but I trust I shall be able to return to you or yours, all that I owe you."

"No obligations at all, my boy!" exclaimed the lawyer. "I remember old scores and I wish you well—you are a wild blade, William, but of a generous strain and I hope you may yet come into your own." He then shook hands warmly, and took his leave.

The young man sat long with bowed head, as if in deep thought, then rose and walked down the pathway, out the gate.

After this night, William Walcott was not seen again at "Bolton House," which stood on a rocky peninsula overlooking Chesapeake Bay, in lower Virginia. This mansion, situated in the midst of farm lands, surrounded by ancient oaks, was the manor house of the estate which had been the marriage portion of his mother, and which should now belong to him as her legal heir. But upon his return from his travels, he had found that his father had married again, and that he himself had been dispossessed of his natural inheritance by the will of his mother. It seemed wonderful that no one had known of the existence of this will until after his father's second marriage. It was equally unfortunate that the officers of the probate court, and all who had had to do with the will had passed away. He pondered over the strange injustice of the act, and the wrong that had been practiced upon him; yet he accepted the opinion of the family lawyer as final, and abandoning his cause, he walked forth into the night, and the darkness inclosed him.

On the following morning the absence of William Walcott from home excited no surprise in the family circle as his habits had been irregular since his return from abroad.

After the lapse of several weeks his friends heard by chance, through the Cunard office in New York, that he had taken passage on one of their ships for Liverpool, bound thence to the gold fields of South Africa.

Amid the gayeties and festivities that were now held under the new régime at Bolton House, the rightful heir to the estate seemed apparently forgotten.

The new mistress of the mansion was youthful and gay, and entertained much company. She required of her servants and dependents that they should address her as "Lady Walcott." But the negro people of the neighborhood persisted in calling her "Miss Frances." This arose perhaps from the circumstance that she would employ none of them about her house, saying, "she had never been used to negroes."

Even had it been otherwise the astounding, mysterious happenings at this residence within the next few months would have dispersed and banished every mother's son of this superstitious race from the premises.

A short time after the disappearance of the young heir of Bolton House, Lawyer Chapman met Miss Kate Beuchtel, the housekeeper to Lady Walcott.

"When will Mr William Walcott return?" said Miss Kate to the lawyer as they met at the post office.

"Indeed, my young lady, I don't know," he replied. "Why don't you inquire of lawyer Guilford, he is the legal light of the family and is expected to know all things."

"Mr. Guilford is not a friend to Mr. William —I know that," she answered.

"Miss Kate is a true friend to Mr. William," said the lawyer, looking her steadily in the eye.

The girl colored painfully, and with a toss of the head, started to move on, but paused and remarked rather saucily: "Yes, I am, Mr. Chapman, and you are too! What do you think now of that will that has just been found, which takes everything away from the poor boy?"

"I think," said Chapman with his accustomed

bluntness, "that it is wrong, and ought not to be allowed to stand!"

"Why then, don't you right this wrong done to your young friend—you are a lawyer!" said the girl warmly.

"Lawyers do not usually try to right wrongs unsolicited," he replied. "Besides, Mr. William has abandoned his own case and left the country, I believe, not to return."

"Don't you think he'll come back after while?" she said in evident distress.

"I do not," answered the lawyer; "he is of a proud nature, and very fixed in his notions."

Tears welled up in her dark eyes as he said this; and she made an effort to speak, but her emotions seemed to choke her utterance.

Finally she replied: "Well, he has one friend left here who will not forget him, and some people will find that out, too, to their long sorrow!"

Then she left the office, and the lawyer marveled much as he noted the flash of fire in her eyes. His reflections were: "That girl has more force of character than I gave her credit for; she may do something yet outside of the commonplace!"

Bolton House was supplied with many modern conveniences, rare even in city residences at the date of this story. A former proprietor, a man of science, had erected a private gas works which furnished light and fuel to the premises. Dumb-waiters and elevators run by water power moved noiselessly between the floors, and speaking tubes communicated with the chambers. The superb dancing hall with waxed floor and brilliant chandeliers was often the scene of revelry. The present proprietor, Thomas Walcott, had followed the sea, and his trim yacht was now moored in a picturesque boathouse, just at the foot of the yard at the head of the inlet. Surmounting the house was an immense glass dome, from which at night shone a great light, the beacon to the harbor.

It was at a ball given just before Christmas by Lady Walcott, in honor of city guests—and to her sister, Miss Celeste Stanley—that a mysterious and startling occurrence took place in the dancing hall.

There were many guests from the city; the large hall was quite full and an excellent band was playing; the night was about half spent and the festivities were at full height when the lights were suddenly extinguished and the hall was left in total darkness!

The surprise was sudden, the silence profound for a few seconds, and then murmurs began to be heard in the vast crowd until a feeble light was visible high up on the middle wall—when exclamations arose—"What is it?" "It's a hand!" "It's on fire!" "What is it writing?"

Then overcome with awe they remained silent as they conned in the flaming letters on the wall, this jingle of rhyme:

> "Read my riddle if you can.
> This house belongs to the younger man."

The hand that wrote shone with some luminous substance, and appeared to protrude from a dim form; and hand, form and inscription all paled and faded away in a few seconds. Yet it seemed altogether miraculous; the crowd was dazed with fear; a few persons near the door ran out and women screamed. Thomas Walcott, a rugged man of sixty years, was seated near one of the large windows in conversation with a lady. He arose and threw up the sash, then in loud, stern tones ordered the servants to bring lights as the gas was filling the room.

When this had been done there was nothing to be seen on the wall, and the scared dancers were more mystified as they began to consider how the lights had been put out while the gas was still flowing through the pipes. This the head servant declared had been the case; the gas plug was in the yard covered with mud and had not been tampered with while the escaping gas pervaded the house.

Thomas Walcott stood for some time after the room had been relighted, gazing at the spot where the inscription had been. It was all too much for this unlearned, seafaring man with much of the sailor superstition in his composition. However, he was brave and even stern when dealing with human affairs, and he now turned to his guests and said: "Friends, I don't understand this, but go on with the dance; this seems some ill-timed trick played by some malicious person to injure me before my friends; do not let it interfere with our merrymaking, but go on with your dance."

The music began and the dance continued, in a half-hearted way, but it was soon over and dancers and guests retired to discuss the startling occurrences of the night.

This affair was almost the sole topic of conversation in the village for several days, and distorted accounts of it appeared in the city papers. The family at Bolton House, however, refused to discuss the subject.

The fact that the former proprietor of this residence had somewhere about the building a laboratory or "ghost room," as they called it, and which had not been found by the present occupants, was given as a circumstance that may have had to do with the apparition on the wall which had terrified the dancers and for which no rational explanation was offered.

Lady Bolton was greatly disturbed at the interruption to the holiday festivities, but concluded to dispel the gloom that was over the place by a grand ball on New Year's Eve. The preparations for the same were very elaborate and many invitations were sent out.

When the eventful evening came the parlors and dancing hall were filled with the élite of society, both of the neighborhood and nearby cities; but it was noticed as a circumstance worthy of remark that many staid people who were present at the first entertainment were now absent.

Even from those present there was many a hurried, scared look directed towards the spot where, on the wall, the mysterious writing had occurred; yet the night waned and nothing happened, nor was like to happen, for in the early evening Thomas Walcott had called to him his handsome housekeeper, Miss Kate Beuchtel, and had remarked significantly that "if there was any more handwriting on the wall it had better be done by a body as thin as that of a ghost or else it would stop a pistol bullet!"

Miss Kate, shortly after that was observed in earnest conversation with two of the house-maids. Meantime everything went well with the dancers—even "charmingly," as one of the young guests remarked to Lady Walcott. Despite all that, exactly as the great clock in the hall-way was on the stroke of midnight—the lights were extinguished absolutely from the gleaming "light-house" in the cupola to the basement story—all was left in utter darkness!

It is difficult to give any adequate expression to the scene that followed—women screamed of course—the fumes of the escaping gas pervaded the house—there was a great rush by the frenzied people for the hall-way—and midway of the hall three young ladies who had a good start and were running out, hand in hand, as if for mutual support—ran plump against an articulated, gleamy skeleton that was dangling from the center chandelier! They fell down in a dead faint and were quiet for the time.

This terrible skeleton without doubt saved their lives; for the frightful object, swaying to and fro, parted the rushing crowd to the right and left of the broad hallway; otherwise these girls would have been trampled to death.

A man came along, and striking a match, lighted one burner of the chandelier to the danger of an explosion; but he noticed that all the windows in the long hallway had been raised. Thomas Walcott, who came next, also noticed this; his fury was unbounded and he seemed a dangerous man; he tore down the skeleton and trampled it to pieces on the tile flooring!

Unfortunately, for him, the next to appear on the scene was the head waiter. He was pale with fright, but grew paler still as Walcott grasped him by the neck, threw him to the floor and would have trampled him under foot had he not been restrained by the men about, as he hissed between his clinched teeth: "What means this tomfoolery—this conspiracy in my house?"

The house was soon relighted, but the guests were thoroughly panic stricken and hastily took their departure without any formal leave-taking.

Lady Walcott retired to her room and was not seen again, even by the servants of the household, for several days. After she became somewhat composed she stated that she and her husband had concluded to return to the city for the remainder of the winter, and in the spring they would have Bolton House repaired and refurnished.

This plan was carried out; they dismissed the servants and retired to the city, but did not take up their residence here again, as they had expected to do. It was not till late in the following May that an architect and house decorators came down to make the needed repairs. As there was no change made in the building, some of the citizens surmised that the architect had been employed that he might through his technical skill discover and explain the mysterious happenings at this house which had given it a bad reputation, and fixed upon it the name of the "haunted house."

If this was the purpose of the architect he signally failed, for a critical examination of the whole premises presented no clue that led to an explanation of the mysteries that overhung the place. After the furnishers and decorators were through with their work, the house was closed again, and so remained until late in the fall. Then word was received that the master and mistress would return on their yacht from a voyage along the coast, accompanied by a few friends, and would make a brief stay at Bolton House. Upon the reception of this announcement, the servants were collected, and the house put in order.

The yacht was to reach her landing at the head of the inlet about nine o'clock on the following Saturday night; all was in readiness, but as it had not arrived at midnight the servants retired, and all the lights were out save the light in the cupola, "the light-house," which was the beacon by which the master was to pilot his craft up the narrow, rocky inlet.

Half an hour later, the greatest crime of the seas was perpetrated—God forbid that any light in any light-house should fail in the midnight and the storm!—yet that is what happened at Bolton House; for, just half an hour after the servants had retired, the great light in the cupola was extinguished, as if snuffed out by a mighty hand! There was no one awake to notice this, and it was not known at the house until after daylight.

But far down the bay, this is what occurred;

half an hour after midnight, the yacht of Captain Thomas Walcott was struggling in a heavy cross-sea, about two knots below the lower headland of the inlet. Walcott himself was at the wheel, his passengers, two ladies and two gentlemen were in the cabin, all very sea-sick; his three seamen were at their posts on deck. This was the situation when the most fearful storm arose that was ever known on Chesapeake Bay.

But Captain Walcott was thoroughly familiar with his surroundings, his craft was a stanch one; he was soon running before the storm under bare poles, and steering by the light in the cupola of his own house. He had every reason to hope that he would make the harbor in safety. Now, while he was holding hard with both hands on the wheel, in tacking, with the wind on his port bow, and the waves washing the deck, his eyes were steadily fixed on the light by which he was steering when it suddenly went out! He let go the wheel with one hand, and rubbed his eyes, as if he could not believe his senses—but the light was gone! and when he realized this—though his heart was sinking —he uttered a substantial oath in cursing "the light that failed!"

He called his oldest seaman to the wheel; he with the other two went to the life-boat, and loosed the tackle in the davits; no questions were asked, the sailors understood, and the passengers in the cabin were unconscious of their danger. These preparations finished, he walked aft and again took charge of the wheel. An hour later, while he was baffling with the seas with rare seamanship, the noble craft was dashed upon a rock, and began to settle down immediately. The passengers rushed out of the cabin in wild dismay, but were met by Walton and his sailors who took possession of them, crowded them into the life-boat without cere-mony—lowered away, cut loose, and put off without the loss of a moment. It was well—for they had barely cleared the vessel when she gave a lurch forward, and went down by the bows beneath the waves in some twenty fathoms of water.

The life-boat with its human freight was now tossing on the rough waters in the inky black-ness of the night. Walcott was at the helm, two sailors at the oars, the third bailing con-stantly to keep afloat; the passengers, one of whom was Lady Walcott, lay helplessly in the bottom of the boat unnoticed by those who were making the brave struggle for life.

All through the weary hours of that night Walcott's brain was troubled with bitter thoughts not unmixed with superstition, as he brooded over the light that had failed him at his utmost need and left him a wreck on the wild waters. He determined if he should escape the

perils that were about him that light should
never be relighted, but remain out forever and
mislead no other mariner on the seas.

The sun was gilding the east when the life-
boat broke through the surf and grated on a
sand bar six miles below Bolton house and half
a mile from a fishing hut. The women were
supported to the hut where some substantial
refreshments were found. The fisherman was
dispatched to the neighboring farm to procure
a vehicle; he returned with a two-horse wagon;
in this the party were conveyed to Bolton House,
arriving there about ten o'clock in the morning
to relate their story of shipwreck and suffering.

No explanation could be made by the servants
why the light had failed, and before the day was
over Thomas Walcott sent to the village for a
mechanic, and all the gas fixtures were removed
from the dome.

The next day the family returned to town;
the servants were discharged, and Bolton House
remained closed. Several weeks later the architect returned and removed the cupola from the
house and remodeled the roof; even then the
mystery was not discovered.

One day late in the fall Thomas Walcott
called at the office of Lawyer Chapman, a circumstance unusual, as they were not on friendly
terms. He took a chair upon invitation and
commenced abruptly—

"You are in correspondence with my son, William, I have been told."

"I have received two or three letters from him since he has been in Africa," the lawyer answered.

"When does he expect to return?"

"I understand that it is his intention not to return at all," was the reply.

Thereupon, Walcott drew forth a legal paper which he requested the lawyer to read.

This he did, seemingly, with great satisfaction, and when he had finished he turned to Walcott and said:

"Captain, that is all right, and I congratulate you heartily upon this just act, but why do you show this to me?"

"As you see," Walcott replied, "this is a deed in fee simple, granting to my son, William, the Bolton House and whole estate which had been the property of his mother. She left this property to me with the verbal understanding that I should transfer it to him upon coming of age. This matter I have delayed to do—being unduly influenced by others; but now I right this wrong and ask you as the friend of my son to write to him and ask him to come home and live among his people, first informing him what I have done."

The lawyer eagerly assented and in his delight at the turn affairs had taken, he gave ex-

pression to one or two unguarded thoughts as
follows: "Miss Kate Beuchtel will be glad to
hear of this, and there will be no more disturbances at Bolton House!"

Walcott looked him sternly in the face and
said: "What had Miss Beuchtel to do with the
disturbances you refer to?"

"I don't know," the lawyer replied hastily,
"perhaps I ought not to have said that, but you
know that she and your son have been lovers
since childhood, and she was very much wrought
up when she heard that he had been dispossessed
of the Bolton property."

"I think myself," the captain replied, "she
had something to do with that matter, but how
that light was put out, I never could fathom."
Then as his thoughts recurred to the scenes of
that night, he continued: "What a mortal sin it
be to douse the light of a beacon on a stormy
night when there be naught to pilot by!"

He spoke with so much feeling the lawyer
was moved to say: "I believe the person who
did that did it without any thought of shipwreck or without any knowledge of the storm
raging on the lower bay at the time. They were
only trying to frighten you, captain."

"Well they did it," he said. And continuing:
"I tell you, sir, we were all nigh unto death for
four hours! Had Bolton light been aglow on
that night my yacht would not now be at the

bottom of the bay!'' As he said this he walked out of the office.

The letter which Lawyer Chapman sent to his young friend, William Walcott, by way of Cape Town, Africa, at the request of his father, contained this paragraph:

"Come home, William, and take possession of your own; the sport is still fine along the old Bay shore; the Club will welcome their gamest sportsman; the finest estate is yours; the prettiest girl awaits your coming; the times are propitious; you cannot tarry!''

*   *   *   *   *

It is needless to say, William Walcott returned to his Virginia home on the receipt of this letter; and a few months thereafter was united in marriage with the beautiful Miss Kate Beuchtel, and that they took up their residence at Bolton House.

Some months later when there was pleasant company at this fine old residence, the young mistress, Kate Walcott, took the old captain by the arm and led him into the ancient library where, after removing books from three shelves, she showed him that this section of the bookcase was hung on three hinges, and on the opposite side of the same section there was a secret spring, which, upon pressing, the whole section of the bookcase swung around, disclosing behind a small door which seemed to open into the jamb of the chimney. Lighting a lamp, the lady opened this door, and ushered the captain into the secret closet of the scientist who once lived here.

It was an uncanny place, cluttered up with specimens of bones, herbs, minerals and chemicals; together with instruments and implements of curious construction. The room was only three and a half feet deep, about six feet wide, and extended in height to the roof; in one corner was a ladder fastened to the wall, which seemed to lead nowhere and to answer no useful purpose; as it stopped midway the wall, which wall was the inner surface of the wainscoting of the dancing hall.

The young lady pointed out to Thomas Walcott the main gas-pipe running through this closet, and showed him the plug by means of which the gas could be controlled without access to the one used by the family in the yard.

She then apologized prettily for having shut off the light from the "light-house," on the night of the storm. "She had done it in her ignorance only to frighten, and not to harm—could she ever be forgiven for that foolish, wicked act!"

She was abashed and troubled as she made the confession, for the grave, stern man smiled, and bowed in silence.

But mustering up her courage as she came to

the lighter comedy, she took up a stick of phos-
phorous from the table of the old chemist, and
climbed the ladder that led to nowhere. When
she was ten feet from the floor she removed a
spring and slid back one of the panels of the
wainscoting, and putting her arm through the
opening she showed the captain how the handwriting had been made on the wall!

Then the old man laughed.

When she came down and rejoined him, he
said: "Well, well, let bygones be bygones. I
always thought there was some conjuring trick
about that, and I have lain awake at night turning that thing over in my thick head, but I
couldn't make it out!"

Then the young woman laughed.

*   *   *   *   *

Thomas Walcott, with the breath of the sea in
his resonant voice, continued: "But my daughter,
that night down on the bay, the blackest night
I ever saw—when there were no moon and
stars—when the wind was blowing a hurricane
and the waves were breaking over the deck—
when I was steering by Bolton Beacon—and the
light went out—I thought the bottom had fallen
out of the world!

"I am an old man and have weathered the
storms of the seas—and though I forgive you
freely—I can never forget The Light that
Failed!"

ON THE TRAIL.

I.

The first "meet" of the fox-hounds of the Redwood Club was held this season at Coverdale, a pretty village nestling among the hills, distant twenty miles from the Club House.

The Club-men had come down the evening previous to the day appointed for the chase, and had made themselves comfortable for the night at the quaint wayside inn. And now the morning of the "meet," after a substantial breakfast by candle-light, they were preparing their "mounts" in the narrow street of the village.

The day had dawned with a fair promise of a successful hunt; the air was moist; the wind was light and southerly; and every true fox-hunter knew "the scent would lay."

One veteran of the chase, as he was tightening the girth of his saddle, gave a searching glance over the back of his "hunter" to the fields and sky, and then remarked: "The pack, on such a day as this, would follow the trail breast high at full speed without putting a nose to the ground."

This was a hearty prophecy to which there

227

was no dissenting voice among the "red-coats" that thronged the street.

The level rays of the rising sun began now to enlighten the animated scene; the master of the hounds wound his horn; and the pack of fifty-two dogs, all spotted, black, white and tan, thorough-bred fox-hounds, gave an answering cry in chorus, yet each in his own peculiar note, which fell upon the ears of the assembled huntsmen as rarest music.

The Redwood Club was composed of fifty members; a choice lot of city men mostly young, but there were a few veterans of the chase among them who had learned to ride under circumstances in which a fall from a horse had been regarded as the least of the dangers that beset them.

When all was ready the master of the hounds wound his horn again, very cheerily, and with the baying of the dogs and the clatter of hoofs the gay cavalcade moved noisily through the village street and was soon afield.

This was the most gallant array of horsemen that had ever assembled at a "meet" of the Redwood Club, and the citizens of Coverdale were correspondingly excited at the unwonted scene.

They proposed to honor the occasion to the extent of preparing a sumptuous dinner for their sporting guests at the close of the hunt. The dinner party was to be held at a private residence which was the most pretentious mansion in the village. However, the entertainment was a town affair, and all who could do so were expected to take part in it, especially the young ladies, as the guests they desired to honor were for the most part young men, the élite of city society.

Sometime after the echo of the horn and the baying of the hounds had died away and the street had resumed its wonted silence, the parson of the village—"'Parson" Dilworth—came driving along together with his friend and guest, Dr. Hooper.

The doctor had come down from the city to attend the "meet of the fox-hounds;" although he was too old a man to ride afield, yet his enthusiasm for the royal sport remained unimpared, and it was his delight to ride, even in his buggy, within sight and hearing of the hounds.

Parson Dilworth, also an aged man, was a most congenial companion for the doctor on such an occasion. He was heard to say to young Vernon—the only member of the club belonging to the village—"I do really love a little manly sport now and then and I fear very much that the modern young man who is content with ball and lawn-tennis is becoming a little too effeminate!"

The parson and Doctor Hooper drove along

the turnpike in the direction taken by the "hunt," and it was their good fortune to come in sight of the "field."

Here they stopped on the ridge as the hunt was bearing away from the road, and as they gazed across the fields they saw the grand "burst" when the fox "broke cover," and heard the stirring cry of the huntsmen: "Tallyho! Gone away! Tallyho! Gone away!"

It was a gallant sight, and they watched the riders under whip and spur as they strove to keep up with the hounds until the outlines of their figures grew dim in the distance and finally disappeared behind an intervening ridge.

They were much elated at the scene, and the parson, who knew the country well, said: "The road takes a turn about a half mile beyond here; let us drive on, we may come in sight of the chase again."

When they arrived at the point indicated by the parson they did perceive two horsemen, one of them a "red-coat" mounted on a splendid chestnut "hunter;" but his companion was not in hunting costume and was mounted on a stocky "roadster;" these horsemen were the only part of the hunt in sight.

The doctor took out his field-glass and looked at them long and steadily; they were gradually approaching the road on a diagonal line, and as the sun broke through a rift in the clouds he discerned them plainly. Thereupon, handing his glass to the parson, he exclaimed:

"Why, bless my life! if that isn't Montague and old Lawyer Wingfield."

"What!" said the parson, "is that Wingfield? Was it not in his city office that death overtook our poor Martin Russel!"

"Yes," was the doctor's reply, "and I never could understand how a narrow soul like Wingfield could find enjoyment in a fox chase; there seems to be something incongruous in the mere fact of his attendance on such sport."

While the two friends conversed the horsemen had drawn near enough to be plainly visible to the naked eye.

Wingfield was a tall, gaunt man who sat his horse in a slouching fashion that ill became the hunting field.

In contrast, Montague, a man of medium stature, was "cast in a mold for manly sports." His hair was iron gray, the only evidence of age noticeable, as he sat his noble hunter with an ease and grace that proclaimed the practiced horseman.

The old parson closed his spyglass very deliberately and remarked: "I have seen that man Wingfield once or twice before and I must say I don't like him! There seems to be some mysterious or malign influence about him."

"I think myself he is a very secretive man," replied the doctor briefly.

"Is that Mr. Montague, the detective, of whom young Vernon was speaking?" queried the parson.

"Yes, that is Col. Montague."

"He is not a young man," observed the parson, "and he seems to have a frank and open countenance. I should have taken him for a manly, generous man, never for a detective."

"Parson, you read men well," answered the old physician. "Montague is not a young man, he is at least fifty, and he is as frank and manly as you have read him: nevertheless, he is a detective, yet something more than a detective."

Just at this time several hounds "opened out" in the covert on the hillside, about two hundred yards in front of the horsemen who were the subject of conversation; and almost immediately thereafter a fox "burst" from the cover, closely pursued by six hounds.

At this, Montague with the cry of "Tally-ho!" put his hunter to speed and rapidly drew on the hounds.

The doctor and the parson as they occupied high ground thought it best to retain their position.

The fox bore straight away holding his own with the hounds and the solitary huntsman in pursuit; for Wingfield could not be said to have a part in the race as he jogged along on his fat roadster.

It was a hot chase; Montague was riding in a gallant fashion and was almost up with the hounds. Reynard, being hard pressed, had turned towards the ridge and the covert on the left, but the cry of a stray hound in the brush had turned him back again, when he continued straight ahead toward the brook, which crossed the line of the chase about fifty yards in advance.

It seemed now that the hounds were gaining on the fox as they approached the "run," but he turned quickly aside and ran across the top rail of a water gate without wetting his "brush;" beyond, he sought the friendly cover of the thick undergrowth which here closed the way.

The hounds in full cry ran straight ahead with noses in air; they plunged into the brook which was full to the banks, and paddling over with whimpering cry were soon lost to view in the thicket.

They were scarcely out of the water when Montague's chestnut hunter at full speed sprang upon the bank, and at one brave bound cleared the brook! But unfortunately the bank broke under him, as he made the leap, and the gallant horse fell prone on the opposite side!

Nothing daunted, his rider with rein and spur lifted him to his feet, and was away before one could realize that he had been down.

Thirty yards beyond the brook there was a rail fence, about five feet high, which enclosed the wood.

Over this fence Montague shot like a red meteor, and disappeared in the underbrush beyond!

The hounds were now running in from all directions and there was a great clamor as the chase bore along the wooded ridge; but as yet none of the huntsmen had come into view.

Twenty minutes later the fox again broke from the covert. There were then a large number of hounds at his heels, and Montague was riding in the midst as straight as a bolt! Thus they ran at a tremendous space for fifty yards until they passed over the ridge and out of sight.

The doctor, all wrought up with excitement, turned to the parson and exclaimed: "There never was a more gallant sight than that! Montague does stir my old blood with his noble horsemanship!"

"He is indeed a fearless rider, I never saw one more so," replied the parson.

"By the way, Doctor," he remarked after a pause, "is this Montague a relative of the cavalry colonel who led the famous charge on the day you were wounded?"

"Why Parson, this is the man himself!"

"O, well then," replied the minister, "I am not surprised at his feats in the hunting field. But I doubt if there is another man in the Club who would have taken the hazard of that leap, while going at such fearful speed."

Then after he had congratulated the doctor

on having witnessed so much of the sport, he turned his vehicle around and drove slowly back towards the village.

As it so happened they were overtaken by Lawyer Wingfield mounted on his fat cob.

"How are you, Doctor? This is a fine day for sport," was his salutation as he rode up.

To this the doctor gave assent by a stiff nod. Wingfield, nothing abashed by his cool reception, began to dilate on the incidents of the chase. The doctor bluntly stopped his harangue by the query:

"Wingfield, you heard the verdict of the coroner's inquest in the case of Martin Russel before leaving town?"

"Of course I was a witness in the case," was the reply. "They returned as their verdict that he had died of apoplexy; there was nothing else to do; the physicians all said he died of apoplexy."

"I did not say so."

"Oh no, Doctor, you testified that you did not know of what he died."

"I may know some day!" was Doctor Hooper's reply.

At this rejoinder a scowl darkened the lawyer's face, as he remarked: "I don't see why you talk to me in this manner, and on an occasion when a more pleasant theme should be the subject of conversation. That fellow, Montague, had the bad taste to broach this subject to me on the hunting field. I want to hear no more of this from you, Doctor; I'll ride on now as I wish to catch the train for the city.''

After he had passed out of hearing the doctor said to his companion: ''He will hear something more from me on this subject whether he wishes to or not, when the proper time comes.''

''Gracious! Doctor, you don't think Martin Russel died an unnatural death, do you?'' queried the parson.

''Parson, I have been a surgeon for fifty years; I have seen a number of fatal cases of apoplexy, and have read of many more: but I never knew a case in which the patient had the constitution, physique and youth of poor Martin Russel.'' And then after a pause, he continued: 'I admit the symptoms were all those of apoplexy, and the young physicians who assisted me in the post mortem had no doubt that was the cause of his death. Yet we old physicians know more than the books—we have our instincts and intuitions that seldom fail, although not always admissible of proof.

''If Russel had been a man past middle age, of florid complexion, short neck, plethoric or of intemperate habits, I myself would have diagnosticated his case as apoplexy.

''As it is, I believe before God that he died an unnatural death; but how he was killed, as he was killed without doubt, I can't explain. Yet on this diagnosis I will stake my reputation as a physician, and with the assistance of Col. Montague I hope in time to be able to solve the mystery. If it is not beyond human ken, he, of all the men I have known, is the one most likely to master the secret. I will tell you this in strict confidence, Parson, you must never say a word about it, not even to Montague himself should you ever have the pleasure to meet him."

The aged minister was silent for several minutes after the doctor had ceased to speak, as though dazed with conflicting emotions; then in a trembling voice, he said: "Doctor, I shall never abuse your confidence; but your words have moved me with painful thoughts. What a wicked world this is, yet the sun has shone fair over our heads this beautiful autumn day, the birds have sung sweetly, and all nature has seemed peaceful. It is hard to realize that man, the lord and master of this beautiful scene and all it contains, can be so desperately wicked, so cruel to his brother man."

As the good man ceased to speak, his horse, apparently without guidance, turned aside and stopped before the gateway to the parsonage, a quaint cottage enclosed in a bower of shrubbery at the outskirts of the village.

The two old friends descended from the buggy and took their seats on the cottage porch as the

level rays of the setting sun shone on the faces
of the returning huntsmen, riding down the village street. The world had turned half around
since the chase had begun and the shades of
night were closing on the pleasant day.

In the earlier part of the chase at Coverdale,
Col. Montague who had fallen to the rear, much
to the surprise of his fellow sportsman, managed
so that in riding to the front again he should
overhaul Lawyer Wingfield, who was also lag-
ging in the rear.

After he had caught up with him, Montague
seemed to be in no haste to go to the front, but
was unusually communicative. In the course of
conversation Wingfield mentioned casually: "I
was late in getting down to the 'meet,' by reason
of being detained at the inquest held over the
remains of Martin Russel."

This gave Montague the opportunity he sought
to hear Wingfield's version of that sad affair.

He said: "Russel had called at my office by appointment made ten days before, to attend to
some legal business; but unfortunately I was detained in Philadelphia on that day and did not
reach my residence in the city until after nightfall, several hours after the dead body of Russel
had been found reclining in my office chair, cold
in death."

"Who first discovered that he was dead?"
queried Montague.

"The janitor, who came to sweep the office at six o'clock in the evening."

"'At what time were you to have met him at your office?"

"At two o'clock p. m."

"When did you first see his dead body?"

"At ten o'clock that night at the coroner's morgue."

"Were there any marks of violence on his person, or any expression of pain in his countenance?"

"None whatever; not in the least; he seemed to have nothing the matter with him except that he was dead!"

"Did the coroner ask you to state your business with Russel that was to have been transacted at your office at that appointment?"

"Yes, fortunately for me, I have a good alibi. I was in Philadelphia—or some mean suspicious person might think that I had something to do with his death."

"You have not answered my question."

"I think I have, Colonel, yet I am not aware that I am under obligations to do so."

"None, except mere courtesy, of course. You know that Russel was my intimate friend, and it is but natural that I should inquire about his death."

"What more do you wish to know about it?"

"I attempted to ask what business took Russel to your office on the day of his death?"

"Well, if you wish to know, it was to divide
a legacy that was bequeathed us by our uncle,
Jethro Scales, of Hartford, Conn.

"You know—or perhaps you don't know—
that Russel and myself were first cousins—it's a
fact, however.

"Well, now, if you are so very particular
about it, this legacy consisted of thirty-nine
thousand dollars in bonds and cash paper, to be
equally divided between us.

"Nobody was so much interested in his living
as myself," he continued, "for Russel had the
custody of the bonds and money, and now that
he is dead, I don't know where they are."

Col. Montague, who was unaccustomed to being
addressed in the tone and manner in which
Wingfield spoke to him, felt all the embarrassment of the situation. But as the fox "broke
cover" about this time, as we have seen, he
gave vent to his feelings by spurring to the
front.

He had food for reflection, and on that evening at sunset as he rode with the fox-hunters
into the village street, he pulled up his horse in
front of Parson Dilworth's to have a word with
Dr. Hooper, in regard to the mystery of the murder which now filled all his thoughts.

The old minister was delighted to take Col.

Montague by the hand; he was quite enthusias-
tic in his expressions, as he recalled the excit-
ing episodes of the chase, of which he and the
doctor had been eye witnesses.

Montague replied: "Oh, sir, these young men
are not quite so sturdy as the doctor and myself, who learned rough riding in the cavalry. A
little brush like that of to-day don't amount
to much, does it, Doctor?"

But not awaiting the reply of the old surgeon,
he motioned him aside, and after an earnest consultation they again approached the preacher,
and informed him that they would be compelled
to return to the city that night. But in the
meantime, they said, they desired to talk over a
matter of great secrecy and also of serious import, in which they would be pleased to have
his advice and counsel.

Thereupon the minister showed them into his
study, but as it was near his supper hour he for-
bade any business until after they had partaken
of refreshments.

The minister's good wife noticed that her
guests were much preoccupied throughout the
meal, despite their polite efforts at sociability.

After supper the parson led them to his library, where Montague presented the doctor
with a small package which was wrapped in oil-
paper, and tied with red tape, such as was formerly used by lawyers in tying legal papers.

The doctor began to open the bundle very deliberately, and while so engaged he stated to the preacher with all seriousness that he and Montague were both of the opinion that Lawyer Wingfield was implicated in some strange way in the murder of Martin Russel. Neither of them doubted that a murder had been committed, and Wingfield, they said, was the only man in the world who would be benefited by his death.

By this time the doctor had unwrapped the parcel, that had been folded and tied with such extreme care. After all, the package contained only an old newspaper; but this the doctor held up before the preacher's face and said: "This paper may carry the seeds of life and death; it certainly contains more information than was ever printed on it.

"Montague got this copy of *The Sunday Register* on the hunting field, from young Vernon, who is his assistant. Vernon is pretty sure he saw Wingfield drop the paper, while riding in the chase, and from the very careful manner in which it was tied up he concluded at once that it was a document of great importance, and immediately presented it to his chief."

Whilst he was talking, the doctor had opened the paper and was scanning its columns with a curious eye.

"Montague informs me, this paper contains 'marks' or 'hieroglyphics,'—that must certainly mean something—where are they, Montague, I don't see them?''

Col. Montague pointed out a marked column that seemed to contain only the notice of a land sale; but in the adjoining column there were a number of blue dots, a single one over a word. These dots were triangular in shape, and had been made most carefully with the point of a blue pencil, specially prepared for the purpose.

"They must mean something," he continued, "for they cost care and trouble to make; so much, that no one would have done this without design."

Thereupon, they all pondered over this column for more than an hour; but the result was discouraging in the extreme. The doctor had set down on a slip of paper all the words over which a blue dot had been placed; but they would make no sense, arrange them as he would. Finally, the parson suggested that he should set down the letters only, over which the blue dots had been placed. This he did and the result was as follows:

"iwillbeonhandonthetenthforrusselandifyouhavelef tathousanddollarsformeinthedrawerthe jobwillbedonebutifathousanddollarsisnotinthedrawernothingwillbedonegypdyce."

This at first view was all Greek to them, but after much perplexity, they straightened out the syllables to read as follows:

"I will be on hand on the tenth for Russel, and if you have left a thousand dollars for me in the drawer, the job will be done. But if a thousand dollars is not in the drawer, nothing will be done!

"Gyp Dyce."

Now, the doctor and Montague both knew of "Gyp Dyce" who was a gypsy doctor, and had frequently been through that part of the country with gypsy bands. He had the reputation of being an educated man and was really a skillful surgeon.

This dark mysterious crime was now made clear to them in a measure, by this communication in cipher. They knew almost beyond a doubt that Martin Russel had been foully murdered, and they believed that Lawyer Wingfield had employed this desperate vagabond to assassinate him, in order that he, Wingfield, might become the only surviving heir to the legacy of thirty-nine thousand dollars, that had been bequeathed them jointly by their uncle Jethro Scales.

Here was a motive indeed, and Wingfield was known to them as an unscrupulous man, especially bold in planning for others to execute. Whilst this was their confident belief, it was by no means clear to them that they could prove that a murder had been really committed; certainly, it was not in their power at present to show the manner in which the cruel deed had been done.

There was an impenetrable mystery about this; it would require an additional autopsy, if it could be shown at all.

Hence, Col. Montague remarked that it would be necessary for the doctor and himself to return to the city on that night.

They felt that they had before them a task that would tax to the utmost the powers of the most skillful of detectives. The men they had to deal with were no ordinary criminals; and to fathom the depth of their plots would require the exercise of an intelligence equal in subtlety to the mind that had planned the inexplicable murder.

The craftiness of the cipher made in the ordinary columns of a newspaper and in such a manner as would pass unnoticed, save to the closest scrutiny, was but characteristic of the dark mind that had plotted this incomprehensible deed.

The old surgeon, Dr. Hooper, with all his long and varied experience, was nonplussed.

"How is it possible," he asked, "to kill a man so as to leave no marks of violence upon his person; no poison in his stomach; no expression of pain on his countenance—to produce an instantaneous and painless death, as if from the visitation of Providence?"

Yet this had been done in the case of Martin

Russel! They felt assured that they knew, from the vague cipher, whom it was that had perpetrated the foul deed : and also, they knew who had instigated the crime.

"How were they now to fasten the guilt upon them?" the old surgeon asked.

"It is first necessary," he said, "for us to discover how the crime had been committed, and the implement or the means employed, that had bereft Martin Russel of his life, and had left him as if apparently enjoying a natural and painless sleep."

During all the subsequent, weary days of their search, the doctor and Montague were ever propounding to themselves the single query : "How, and by what means did Gyp Dyce kill Martin Russel?"

II.

When a man dies in the vigor of manhood from some explainable cause, dragged down to his grave, it may be, by the burden of disease, or else cut off by calamitous accident, his death entails upon his relatives only that natural grief and mourning that come to all humanity, soon or late. But if he shall die as did Martin Russel—"the picture of health and strength"—a sudden, mysterious, unexplainable death—to the natural grief of his taking off, there is added an element of harrowing suspicion that tortures his stricken relatives and friends with a disquietude that only the revelation of the mystery can allay.

It was such feeling that had prompted Col. Montague, a lawyer, to play the part of a detective for a time, in his endeavor to unfold the dark mystery that surrounded the death of his friend.

The old surgeon, Dr. Hooper, who had served at the coroner's inquest, while consenting that the jury should return as their verdict: "Death from some unknown cause," yet firmly believed that Russel had been murdered, although his remains had borne no tangible evidence of a violent death.

The doctor had not consented to this verdict through any desire to conceal crime, but rather, to facilitate its discovery. Russel was his friend also, and he never for a moment thought to relinquish the search until the murderer had been discovered.

As a man of science he was also deeply interested in discovering the manner of the murder.

The younger surgeons at the inquest believed, as already stated, that the death of Russel was most probably the result of apoplexy; yet because of the doubtful nature of the case they also agreed to the above verdict.

Martin Russel, a native of Coverdale, had come to Wheeling when a mere lad, and had found, as good fortune directed, a position as office boy in the office of Richard Montague. From him, he had won such favors, as the years had passed, that by his generous aid he had been enabled to attend the public schools where he had received a practical, useful education, and was in the meantime guided by his friend in the study of the law; so that on becoming of age, he was admitted to practice in the city courts.

Step by step he had risen from obscurity to the honorable position of City Attorney. But the Civil War intervening, both he and his friend, Montague, had lain down their "briefs" and taken up the sword.

In the course of this war Col. Montague had won such great renown as had completely eclipsed and overshadowed the honorable record of all his previous endeavors. Martin Russel, too, had won fame as a captain while serving in Col. Montague's regiment.

Thus the friendship of these men became cemented. They had endured together the toils and sufferings of the soldier's life, and they respected each other for the dangers they had passed in common.

We have seen the conspicuous part that Col. Montague bore in the chase of the Redwood hounds at Coverdale; but his chief object in being present on that occasion was to follow a trail other than that of the fox—one in fact, which he was to follow for months.

He was, however, a zealous lover of the chase, and on that occasion his eager spirit had been moved by the opportune incidents narrated; so that for the time, forgetting his errand there, he gave himself up entirely to the joyous excitement of the moment—and rode to the front on that field of rural sport as he had ridden on other fields, where the bugle's call, and not the hunter's horn, had rallied the horsemen.

*   *   *   *   *

In the coroner's morgue in the city a bright light shone during all the silent watches of the night after the chase at Coverdale.

Here, Dr. Hooper, assisted by a surgeon, an expert in brain diseases, was holding a second autopsy in making a critical examination of the skull and brain of Martin Russel; for the elder surgeon insisted that the injury that had caused his death, if any existed, would be found somewhere "in the organism of the nerve tissues of the brain."

Patiently and silently they labored, while Col. Montague, seated nearby, was a spectator to the ghastly scene.

It was two o'clock in the morning when Dr. Hooper with an exclamation of surprise called the younger surgeon to his side. Together they used the microscope freely, and after a long discussion, the old physician extracted some minute particle from the mass of the brain before him, and then turning to Montague, said: "We have found it!"

The colonel arose and walked to his side and at his request looked through the surgeon's microscope, and saw in a magnified form an object which he was enabled to discern with his naked eye — a small steel point like that of a cambric needle about one-sixteenth of an inch in length.

This had been imbedded in the brain of the victim! "This foreign substance," said Dr. Hooper, taking it up with his tweezers, "caused the death of poor Russel!

"It has been shot into his brain by some powerful force," he said, "through the foramen magnum, destroying the medulla, the nervous center, and causing immediate death. See, this little bit of steel is newly fractured; besides, the man could not have lived for two seconds after this had punctured the medulla.

"The movements of respiration are performed partly by the diaphragm and partly by the intercostal muscles and are differently modified by injuries of the nervous system according to the spot at which the injury is inflicted. If in this instance the spinal chord had been divided or much compressed in the lower part of the neck, the intercostal muscles would necessarily have been paralyzed and his respiration would have been diaphragmatic.

"If on the other hand the phrenic nerve had

been divided, the diaphragm would have been paralyzed and his respiration would have been then what is termed 'thoracic' or 'costal'.

"If the injury had been inflicted on the spinal chord alone, just above the origin of the second and third cervical nerves, both the phrenic and intercostal nerves would have been paralyzed and death would necessarily have taken place from suffocation. But in these cases the attempt at respiration would have been manifested by the distended mouth and nostrils of the subject, which was not the case.

"It is a matter of some comfort to us to know that he died a painless death. For this steel point which must have been at the extremity of a curved needle, eight or nine inches long, was driven so forcibly through the foramen magnum that it punctured the medulla oblongata.

"Here the reflex actions, which I have just mentioned, all take place; hence both the power and the desire to breathe were at once taken away. He made no attempt at inspiration; there was no struggle and no appearance of suffering. The man died simply by a want of aeration of the blood which led to the arrest of his circulation. His death was instantaneous with the blow."

Col. Montague inferred from all this without following very closely the doctor's technical disquisition, that his poor friend, Martin Russel, had been foully dealt with by some unknown person, who had been concealed in Wingfield's office with the design of putting him out of the way.

He remembered the stress Lawyer Wingfield had placed on the circumstance that "he could prove an alibi," and also with what precision he had made known his absence from his office at the very time he was in honor bound to have been present to have kept his engagement with Russel.

He believed these facts justified him in entertaining the opinion that Wingfield, himself, had planned the murder, though it was not his hand that dealt the cowardly blow which had driven the stiletto to the "vital point," the center of the nerve origin, stopping at one fell blow all the functions of the living body!

The assassin who directed this blow must have possessed an intimate knowledge of human anatomy, and more than that, the hand that had guided the strange weapon must have been the steady, trained hand of a most skilful surgeon!

Col. Montague and Dr. Hooper were unremitting in their efforts to ferret out the mystery of the murder. The "cipher letter" in the newspaper was convincing to their minds that Wingfield had been the instigator and evil plotter of the deed. And though they now had positive proof that a murder had been wrought, yet they

felt it would be next to impossible to fix the
guilt on him through the vague uncertain communication of the cipher which had caused them
such trouble to unravel. Even if they had made
no mistake in their interpretation of it, this
secret communication nowhere bore the name of
"Wingfield."

Young Vernon, who had picked up the paper
in the hunting-field, said: "He felt sure that he
had seen Wingfield drop it, but as there were
other horsemen near that spot at the time, it was
not impossible for him to be mistaken."

It is true they could prove that he had died
in Wingfield's office; that he had been killed by
an anatomist thoroughly familiar with his human
subject; they could show the point of the
needle that had punctured the medulla oblongata of the victim and caused his instant death

If they could have procured the arrest of Gyp
Dyce, the gypsy doctor who had devised the
cipher and whose hand, no doubt, had directed
the instrument of death—they then might have
been able to implicate Wingfield with the
crime.

But Gyp Dyce had disappeared as mysteriously
as he had come, and the only evidence that he
had ever held any communication with Wingfield
was the unreliable, indefinite, "cipher letter."
Even this would be denied successfully, unless
they could show beyond all controversy that the

"cipher" had really been in the possession of Wingfield.

Col. Montague had employed detectives to search the gypsy bands far and near, all in vain; for Gyp Dyce was never seen again in Wheeling.

Could they only discover the implement or means by which the murder had been done!— and where was the "drawer" in which Wingfield was to have placed —and no doubt did place—as the "job" was "done"—the "thousand-dollars?"

A search of the law-office of Wingfield might produce some clew to the mystery, but how was this to be brought about? It would not do for them to bring a charge of murder against him, until they could substantiate it.

But time, which ends all things, also put a period to this mystery; but all too late to encompass the ends of justice.

It was about three years after the death of Martin Russel that old Lawyer Wingfield was stricken with pneumonia, complicated with fever, and died within two weeks.

Then Dr. Hooper and Col. Montague began to think that the mystery, on the trail of which they had been plodding with unflagging zeal, would never be revealed. But they did not despair entirely, for Montague had obtained permission from the administrators of Wingfield's estate, to search among the books and papers in his office. He had hopes of finding there some clue that would lead to the unravelment of the mystery.

For many days he had searched in that dingy office, over dusty shelves and drawers, and examined bundles of musty law papers, without avail.

There came a time when he was wearied with his labors, and had seated himself beside an antique table, and was thrumming idly thereon. His attention was soon attracted to the peculiar sound made, as if the table contained a drawer —for on tapping on a table with a drawer, the confined air within makes a sound entirely different from that made under similar conditions, when one taps on a table without a drawer.

Now, the only remarkable thing about this was, this table contained no drawer apparently, although the "sound" proclaimed that it did.

He took a searching look about it, and pulled at the sides all around, yet found do drawer. Then it occurred to him that he would better look under the table anyhow; this he did by stooping down and peering beneath, as it was very low; when, sure enough, there was a drawer!

Sound, in this instance, had been truer than sight. The question now was, how he should find an opening to the drawer; he spent a full half hour in fruitless efforts to do so, pulling at the sides and lifting at the top, until he was almost tempted to take a hatchet and split it open.

But on looking more closely at the inner sides of the legs, up near the lid, he discovered on one of them a spot about the size of a thumb-print, which appeared of somewhat lighter color than the paint and also somewhat raised.

On this spot he pressed and found it was a spring that moved; this he compressed and at the same time tried to tilt the top by taking hold of the sides, without effect. Then still compressing the spring, he tried to lift the corners and at the third corner the top tilted and the drawer was opened easily; the top was hinged to the opposite diagonal corner.

Within the drawer there was nothing except an implement, somewhat like a large metal match safe, yet it was easy to be seen it was not a match box; for on its sides there was a small wheel and rachet, on the former a diminutive handle to turn, with the evident design of compressing a spring.

Whilst Montague was examining this curious instrument, he noticed Dr. Hooper, who at that moment was passing the office; he hailed him and invited him to enter.

The old surgeon came in, thumping his heavy cane on the floor, all the while glancing around from beneath his shaggy brows, as if in search of something lost.

"Doctor, I want to show you a curious piece of furniture," Montague said, as he walked to the antique table. "You see this table has no drawer," turning it around. "Now, look, you see it has a drawer!" as he pressed the spring and tilted the top.

"Well! Well!" exclaimed the physician, "if that isn't a rascally piece of furniture—did you find anything in it?"

"Yes, this implement; I don't know what it is—you will have to explain it," said Montague.

The doctor took it in his hand, turned it over carefully, then said: "I think it must certainly be some kind of lancet, and it is already set; now look out! I've found the spring, and will let it off;" then he pressed a little button, and out flew with great force—a thin curved wire-like lancet, with the point broken off.

The old surgeon gazed on it aghast and silent; then, when he could recover himself, he said sternly: "This is the accursed implement that killed Martin Russel!"

Montague, on examining it was satisfied of that too: but the doctor to make assurance doubly sure, hobbled down to his office and soon returned with the bit of steel which he had extracted from the brain of Russel and found that it exactly fitted the point of this stiletto!

Old Doctor Hooper was greatly excited by the

discovery; he set the "lancet," as he called it, many times and "shot it off."

"This accursed instrument," he said, "was made in the old world, perhaps in the dark ages; no man in this new country would ever devise such a weapon to slay his enemy with; this devil's-dagger came from a land rife with tyranny, cruel oppression, torture and secret murder!

"But this murder of Russel is the most scientific assassination that has ever been perpetrated in this country!" he continued; "no man, except a thorough anatomist, one with iron nerves as well as the technical knowledge, could have directed the fatal blow to 'the vital knot.'

"The victim's life was snuffed out as a candle: as surely, as painlessly, and as noiselessly; there is no parallel to this murder in all the annals of crime!

"We should gain great applause to ourselves by making plain to the world the dark and subtle ways of the learned murderers. But as Wingfield, the arch assassin is dead, we must not reveal our discovery to anyone, for the sake of his innocent wife and children. We must search the world over for Gyp Dyce, and if we shall find him, then we shall make all known in order to encompass the ends of justice."

Several years passed away and Dr. Hooper and Col. Montague continued on the trail of the "gypsy-doctor" until it led to a lone camp in the far west, where that accomplished villain had yielded up his own life to the stiletto; yet in a much less skillful way than that by which he had taken the life of Martin Russel; for he was stabbed to death, with many wounds, by his wild associates in a drunken brawl.

After they had learned this, Montague and Dr. Hooper ceased their labors.

However, they continued to observe the strict silence which they ever maintained in regard to their discovery; for they would bring no distress of mind to the innocent relatives of Wingfield through any effort to vaunt their own skill, as shown in the unravelment of the intricacies of the mysterious murder.

It was only through the writings of Dr. Hooper published many years after his death, that the details of the murder of Martin Russel became known to the medical profession.

TRELAWNEY,

OR THE MYSTERIES OF THE TAGGART HOUSE.

I.

Opposite the town of Clonmel, now in West
Virginia, and on the bank of a rugged mountain stream, stood an ancient time-stained house
which, in its day, had been the most pretentious
residence in all that country side. A tall portico extending the whole length of the main
building and supported by six massive Doric
columns, gave rather an official aspect to the
mansion. This house was marked by another
feature more common to public than to private
residences: an antique cupola in which hung an
equally antique bell, surmounted the building.
The bell had been silent for many years, but the
times were in the prosperous days of old, when
morning, noon and night its silvery notes had
rung out afar, across hill and dale.

This house was for many generations the home
of the Taggart family, and was surrounded by a
plantation of a thousand acres of fine arable
land. The men of this family had been noted
for their great energy and enterprise, and had
pretty much dominated affairs in this part of

the country. But the last of the race had passed away and the estate had fallen into the hands of a collateral branch which did not occupy it; but had leased it, together with the mansion, for many years previous to the happening of the remarkable events here recorded.

Even in the time of the Taggart family there were uncanny stories, told by the negroes of the plantation, of ghostly sights and sounds, seen and heard within the gloomy recesses of the old manor house; but at that time, these stories were attributed to African superstition, and made but little or no impression upon the more intelligent white citizens of the community.

It is necessary to go back to a period several years anterior to the opening of this story, and to recount briefly the dreadful occurrences of that time, which incidentally as it were, nevertheless cast an indelible glamour of horror upon this ancient house.

Towards the close of a beautiful October day, in the year of grace 1826, two horsemen might have been seen riding along the road in the direction of the town of C. and at a distance of about three miles from that place. These travelers were men somewhat past middle age; and he who rode in front would have arrested attention even within a crowded city, much more upon a lonely, country road.

He was apparently about sixty years of age,

but still vigorous, tall and elegantly formed; his complexion was very dark, as if from exposure to a tropical sun; his eyes were piercing, black, roving and fierce of expression: his nose was acquiline; his face long and oval; his locks, which fell upon his shoulders, were streaked with grey as were his moustache and the thinner beard upon his bronzed cheeks. He sat his horse with ease and grace which is acquired only from long practice in the saddle; yet there was a military stiffness and dignity of bearing about the man which he seemed to be unable to shake off, or, perhaps it was that air of authority which attaches to those who have been long accustomed to command.

The horse of this rider was as remarkable in appearance as himself; he was a powerful animal, with a clean, high head, pointed ears, thin mane and tale, and of a curious tawny color, marked upon the sides and flanks with stripes, in less degree but somewhat resembling those of a tiger.

The other traveler was a man of medium height compactly built; of sandy complexion, red hair and beard; goggled eyed; and there was nothing about him to attract attention except his foreign dress, and the very fine animal he rode. The horses of these travelers were evidently of a strain then uncommon in this part of the world, and showed at every point their Arab origin.

It was about nightfall when the elder man, who rode in front, turned to his companion and said: "Symonds, the day is far spent and Saracan is leg weary; we shall stop at the first shelter."

"If it please you, sir" replied the one addressed, as he raised his hand to his hat in military salute, and then relapsed into silence.

But a short time thereafter a turn in the road brought into full view of the travelers a habitation which appeared to be some kind of a fortification or fort, as the square of rude cabins was surrounded by a strong, high picket fence except immediately in front, where the pickets had been removed and replaced by a rail fence about five feet high. As they came nearly opposite to this fort the elder traveler, without a word, reined up his horse and turned off the road at a trot: he rode directly at the fence, which his horse cleared as lightly as the swallow skims the wave. Now Peter Luttrell, the master of the house, who was standing in his doorway at the time, was filled with admiration at this feat of horsemanship.

The stranger stated briefly his needs and craved hospitality for the night; he spoke with a full pleasant voice, but with a foreign accent and a slightly lisping speech. "He was James Trelawney, and his companion, John Symonds; they were from foreign parts, strangers, traveling through the country." Further than this he made no statement concerning himself.

"If you can put up with our humble fare, I shall be pleased to accommodate you," replied Luttrell heartily, and with old Virginia courtesy hastened to assist the stranger to dismount.

By this time Symonds who had ridden around to the gate approached and he and Luttrell took the horses to the stable at some distance from the dwelling.

Trelawney walked into the house as directed; saluted the woman there with grave courtesy; took the chair which she had placed for him, and sat in silence. But he was not unobserved, and from what occurred afterwards all these unimportant details were matters of absorbing interest, as related to the neighbors by Mrs. Luttrell who described in detail the dress and manner of Trelawney.

"Has not this house been used as a fort of some kind?" asked Trelawney, as they sat at the supper table, noticing the small portholes in the logs.

"Yes" replied Luttrell, "we had a good deal of trouble with the Indians here a little over thirty years ago; and this is one of the log forts in which our neighbors used to collect when they were making a raid in this section. However, we have had no fight with them since the great treaty, in the year ninety-five, when the

Redskins promised to keep the peace, "'as long as the sun shall set in the west;' and I reckon, sir, they are gwine to do it," he concluded.

"There ought to be plenty of game in this country," remarked Trelawney, "as it seems to be pretty much all woods."

"Yes indeed, sir," said his host, "this is a great game country; it was the big hunting ground of the Indians; they never lived here, only came here to hunt, and that's what made them fight like the devil before they would give it up."

"You cannot blame them much," said the stranger.

"Oh no," replied Luttrell, "I don't blame them, but I used to shoot at them when I was a boy. I got that mark on my cheek thar when I was fighting the red devils at the fort over on the creek."

Mrs. Luttrell noticed that Trelawny gave a quick glance at the scar on her husband's cheek and from this time forth that he treated him with deference which pleased her greatly, as coming from a man of such distinguished presence, and so different from any she had ever seen. She longed too to inquire how he had received one or two scars that marked his own bronzed face, but did not care to do so.

After the frugal repast was ended, the travelers sat around the huge wood fire and smoked their pipes while Luttrell recounted to them various anecdotes of his hunting adventures in the surrounding mountains.

At length Trelawney expressed a desire to stop over on the morrow for the purpose of taking a deer hunt. Luttrell eagerly encouraged him to carry out this design, as the grave stranger had won much upon his favor. He promised to have guns and everything in readiness at daylight, as the travelers had expressed a desire to return to the house in time to proceed to the town on the following evening.

With this understanding the strangers were shown to their place of rest, which was in an out-building standing at some distance from the main house, and in the direction of the stables. Here they found a small cabin containing two beds; and while all things within were rude and humble, they were at least comfortable, and the travelers expressed themselves well contented with their quarters.

May they rest well! as this may be the last night on earth in which they shall repose in untroubled sleep; for the heavy hand of misfortune is hanging over them, as the sword hung over Damocles, ready to fall and destroy.

As we shall see, the acts and words of these strangers while they remained at the house of Luttrell, were afterwards subjects of the deepest interest to the people of this vicinity, and even called forth the closest scrutiny the law could command. We shall now leave them to their rest, and turn to the events of this night at a point not far distant; and to that terrible tragedy which filled this peaceful country side with horror, and enveloped these strangers within its baneful shadow.

II.

It was ten o'clock and the night was dark and lowering although the gibbous moon hung high in the heavens, and at rare intervals cast a gleam of light to earth between the scurrying clouds. At a point on the road called "The Narrows," about half way between Luttrell's and the town, and which is about a mile from either place, there is a gloomy and narrow passage between the hill and the creek, of some fifty yards in length. A stranger traveling this road after nightfall would hesitate to pass through such a dark and forbidding way; yet there were those, it seems, who had sought this place in which to tarry for good or ill; for by the uncertain light of the moon, the dim outlines of dark figures were to be seen upon horses about midway of this passage, where a small stream trickled down from the hill.

There they sat, silent and motionless, facing the road. After a time the moon shone out;

although dimly, it was reflected from the barrel
of the long pistol which each figure held in his
right hand, and rested on the mane of his horse.

Fifteen minutes passed, and no sound from
man or beast; only the hooting of an owl on
the hillside had broken the stillness. And so
the half hour passed, and the hour, and still no
change or movement.

Will these figures never move or make a sound,
or are they only a figment of the imagination?

For what purpose would armed men station
themselves on this deserted road at the dead
hour of the night, where none do pass?

But even now, in the far distance is heard
the faint sound on the stony road, of a horse's
hoofs; nearer it comes, and louder the sound;
evidently, it is some traveler riding at a round
trot towards the town.

As the ringing hoofs resound at the entrance
to the narrow way, one of the waiting figures, he
on the right, comes to life as it were; turns his
head as if upon a pivot, and nods to the figure
on his left, who nods in return.

Then their long pistols are raised and extended
over the horses' heads, pointing across the road.

On comes the traveler without slacking his
pace, until a stern "Halt!" causes him involuntarily to pull up his horse and turn his face in
wild alarm toward the rock, whence the sound
seems to come; but only for a second was the

suspense, when two pistol shots rang out on the night air, and the fated rider plunged headlong from his horse to the ground; then rolled over and lay upon his back with his face turned up to the dim light of the moon, while the blood flowed rapidly from a ghastly wound in his head.

The work of the assassins has been well done; this traveler, whoever he be, has finished his journey!

But, perhaps the robbers did not premeditate murder, for as the shots were fired, a gruff voice called out—"Job, what made you shoot?"

"What made you shoot?" was the reply; "well, he'd a knowed us anyhow; he'll not talk now," the voice continued.

The highwaymen then made a fruitless attempt to catch the riderless horse which ran past them, down the road, in the direction of the town; but they themselves, after they had robbed the dead man of money and papers, departed in the opposite direction.

The sun was an hour high on the following morning when a countryman dashed into the town of C. with the startling intelligence that Richard Hinton, ex-sheriff of the county, had been foully murdered and that his body lay in the "narrows of the road on the creek!"

It was not long before the whole male population of the town had gathered about the spot where the tragedy had occurred.

Hinton was a man past middle age, and as his children were all grown, there was none present to mourn his sad taking off with that violent outburst of grief with which the young bewail sudden death. Yet the whole community was deeply moved, as no murder had occurred in this quiet neighborhood within a generation. Hinton was known personally to every one in this part of the country; an ex-sheriff and a trusted man; he was just on his return from Richmond with land warrants and considerable sums of money belonging to citizens of the town.

As his pockets were turned wrong side out and there was not left on his person any article of value, not even his old silver watch, it was the consensus of the assembled wisdom that he had been murdered for the purpose of robbery.

After the remains had been removed with all tenderness and rude ceremony to the town, and the excitement had somewhat subsided, those who had met pecuniary loss by the tragedy began to feel a lively interest in discovering the perpetrators of the murder.

The sheriff's *posse comitatus* soon discovered the place where the robbers sat on their horses and from which they had shot their victim. Step by step they trailed the horse tracks up the road until they led into the stable at Luttrell's.

Here, the party were greatly surprised to find two horses, the finest they had ever seen! and wonder of wonders! there were on each saddle, holster pistols, and the right-hand pistol of each holster had been recently discharged while the pistols in the left holsters were still loaded! And more than that, a land warrant belonging to Col. Donovan, and which Hinton was to bring from Richmond, was found stuffed into one of the holsters alongside the pistol!

Could any case be clearer than this; surely the foul murderers had but illy concealed their tracks! Where were the owners of these fine horses who had killed Hinton and had even carelessly left one of his land warrants with their saddles!

Mrs. Luttrell told the sheriff and his party all about the strangers, her guests, describing them minutely, and at the same time she stated that they would return from the hunt about three o'clock, when she was to have dinner prepared for them so that they could go on to the town that night.

The sheriff concluded to conceal his party in a thicket near by and await the return of the strangers, when he would make the arrest.

Col. Donovan, a bluff, hearty man of middle age, was one of the party, and he was the only one of it who was not convinced that the owners of the horses were the murderers. He said to some of his companions while they lay in concealment:

"Boys, this won't do; this is a put up job; these men would never ride back here after such a murder and then go off for a deer hunt—this is against human nature!"

"Colonel, you may know more about the law than we do," was the reply, "but we can't help being governed and convinced too, by the evidence of our senses!"

The hunting party returned at the time they had appointed and the strangers seemed elated at their fine success in the chase. They were allowed to enter the dwelling and were seated at the dinner table when the sheriff led his party, unseen, up to the side of the house near the door. Then he and one other entered.

The sheriff approached rapidly and caught the elder stranger, Trelawney, by the collar of his coat, exclaiming:

"You are my prisoner, you bloody murderer!"

Trelawney, without a word but with a dark scowl on his countenance, sprang up, and the next instant the sheriff lay sprawling on the floor from a blow of his fist. The man who went to his assistance met the same fate; but the party at the door rushed in and displayed their weapons and the strangers were compelled to surrender.

In fact the man Symonds, the companion of

Trelawney, had not attempted to move, but had sat as if dumbfounded, with his eyes bulged out as if they were about to drop from their sockets.

After things had quieted down a little and all the belongings of the strangers had been collected and their horses made ready to go to the town, Trelawney turned and thanked Luttrell and his wife for their hospitality and at the same time took out some money to pay them.

But the sheriff would not permit this; he ordered the prisoners to be searched and everything of value taken from them, which was done.

Trelawney then sternly demanded "by what authority he was arrested; and what kind of people they were, who with arms and force of numbers thus maltreated strangers?"

He spoke with the foreign accent and lisping speech, before remarked, and it was also noticed by the party that he was a man well advanced in years.

The sheriff who was still smarting under the blow he had received, replied coarsely: "You will find out what you are arrested for, you bloody murderer, when you come to swing on the gallows!"

"Tut, tut, sheriff," said Col. Donovan, "the man is innocent until he is proven guilty."

At this, Trelawney turned and bowed with grave courtesy to Col. Donovan, but he spoke not again.

The prisoners then, after a brief examination before the village magistrate, were remanded to jail to await the action of the grand jury at the November term of court. But as the whole community, with the exception of Col. Donovan, and one or two other lawyers, had already decided upon their guilt, some of the more hotheaded citizens insisted on hanging them then and there, and thus save the expense of a trial. But this rash counsel did not prevail.

III.

Now the ill repute of the old Taggart house was greatly enhanced by its connection with this dark tragedy, brought about in the following manner: For some time previous to the trial of Trelawney and Symonds for the murder of Hinton, a new court house was building in the town. The clerk's and sheriff's offices had been moved to this ancient mansion temporarily; and here it was decided to hold the November term of the court.

The judge's stand was placed inside the doorway of one of the ancient rooms, facing the hall, and just leaving room enough for the jury to be seated to the right and left of the door, while the spectators must be content to occupy the hall and the large portico.

Here the trial was held which from its appalling attendant circumstances was afterwards the

subject of conversation about many a winter fire-
side, where the youthful listeners were chilled
with horror at the recital of the ghostly stories
which relegated the "haunted house" to the do-
main of spooks and wraiths and those unearthly
apparitions that are believed to take possession
of ancient houses, where some cruel injustice or
grievous wrong has been perpetrated, and which
needs to be righted.

When the trial came on, Colonel Donovan was
appointed by the court to defend the prisoners.

As all their effects had been taken from them,
and deposited in the bank by the sheriff for safe
keeping, it was not known that they had funds
of their own with which to employ counsel.

The inhabitants of the whole country were assembled at the Taggart house on the day of trial,
many coming two or three days' journey through
the wilderness to witness this famous case.

However, the trial did not continue very long,
for it took only half a day to empanel a jury;
and the whole case was concluded within three
days.

The testimony elicited by the prosecuting attorney was the same as already known. It was
proven to the satisfaction of every one that the
murderers of ex-sheriff Hinton had ridden to
the place of the murder on the horses owned by
the prisoners.

It was further proven beyond a doubt, that

the weapons used were the holster pistols belonging also to the prisoners.

Two shots had been fired, and two of the holster pistols were found to be unloaded; besides, a wad picked up at the scene of the murder exactly fitted the pistols, which were all of the same foreign pattern. Moreover, a bullet of the same gauge was extracted from the body of the dead man; and this together with the damning evidence of the land warrant, found in one of the holsters, and known to have been upon the person of Hinton, brought conviction to almost every mind, of the guilt of the prisoners.

The able attorney for the prosecution stated that in the course of his long practice, he had never before had a case of so much importance, that really proved itself and needed no argument; and that for his part, he would be perfectly willing to submit the case to the jury without a word of comment.

Col. Donovan, for the defense, was unable to disprove the testimony already detailed; he was compelled to admit that the prisoners' horses were ridden by the murderers; and that their pistols had been used to commit the crime; but he contended that these were facts disconnected from the prisoners, and that some other persons, not they, had killed Hinton.

He reviewed in detail the testimony of Luttrell and his wife, repeating every word and describing every act of the prisoners, from their first appearance in the neighborhood, up to the time of their arrest.

But here, he was interrupted by the state's attorney, who stated that there was one fatal omission; and that was the time which elapsed between nine o'clock at night—the time at which the strangers had retired to rest in the cabin, which was nearer the stable and the road than was Luttrell's house—and the hour of five o'clock in the morning, when Luttrell had awakened them for the chase. Here were eight hours when the strangers were unobserved by anyone, and no doubt this was the time within which the murder had been committed. Luttrell admitted on the witness stand that his guests might have taken out their horses and ridden down the road in the night without his knowledge.

But the prosecutor neglected to add, that Luttrell on leaving the stand had volunteered the statement, "he did not believe they did."

Col. Donovan resumed: "Not one cent of money or one article known to have belonged to Hinton, was found on the persons of the prisoners; only, the land warrant belonging to myself, and which was placed in the holster by the unknown murderers with the deep design of throwing suspicion on my innocent clients. For the same subtle purpose, the horses had been used by the murderers, and then had been returned to their stables in the dead hour of the night, so that in the morning light the trail might lead directly to these defenseless strangers. Where then, are the murderers? God only knows, they are not here!"

"I think they are here, and pretty safely here!" interrupted the state's attorney.

By the remark Col. Donovan seemed to be much disturbed, and it was with strong emotion he said: "The lips of the accused are sealed, they cannot speak for themselves." Then pointing to Trelawney, he continued; "But there is a language of nature written in the human countenance, more powerful than spoken words, and the hand Immortal never traced cowardly crime on the bold features of that man!"

Donovan paused, trembling with excitement; then, after wiping his moist brow, he continued: "The flippant remarks of the attorney for the prosecution are, unfortunately, not characteristic of himself alone, but of his class.

"Prosecutors feel called upon to convict. Yet why should this be so? Why should the shield of the law be removed from the breasts of defenseless strangers, and the sharp spear of the law turned against them?

"Trelawney and his companion are here, in the toils of the law, friendless and alone. But I can recall one of that name who, in the olden time, had a better following; and I am also reminded by the song and the old refrain

"'And shall Trelawney die?
Here's twenty thousand Cornishmen
Will know the reason why!'

"Men love power and are swayed and moved
by its influence as the winds move the waves of
the sea. Had my unfortunate friend such a
following as the Trelawney of the song,
this state's attorney would be peradventure, as
obsequious in his bearing, as he is now insolent
and intemperate in his language towards him.

"There has not been developed on this trial
one scintilla of testimony except circumstantial
evidence, which is entirely unsupported by direct testimony. You have heard many cases
cited in this trial which have been decided upon
circumstantial evidence alone.

"You have heard in these cases that the jur-
ies had been mistaken; the courts had been
mistaken; and irreparable wrong had been perpetrated against innocent men.

"Do circumstances speak so loud and so sure
in this case that you cannot be mistaken? Are
you prepared, on such evidence, to condemn
these prisoners to death, to take away the vital
spark? It is so easily done; it is so quickly
done; yet when it is done, despite the skill of
mortal surgery, it is forever done!

"The state's attorney says the murder of
Richard Hinton must be avenged.

"These prisoners are here, strangers and

friendless; it is always safe to condemn to death the stranger and the friendless; for after their death there will be none to remember their wrongs; they will be forgotten!

"But may God forget me when I need help, if I should ever consent to use the quibbles of the law to hamper to their destruction the steps of innocent men!"

Then Col. Donovan walked up close to the jury box and shaking his hand in the faces of the jurors, continued with great earnestness:

"Should you, relying on these flimsy circumstances, condemn these men to death—I take a long look ahead to that time when I, and these old men hereabouts have been gathered to our fathers—to that time when the revelation shall have been made to you, younger men of this jury—that you have been mistaken—that Trelawney and Symonds were innocent men!

"I draw the veil over the scene to conceal the remorse and recrimination of that time, and speak no more on this subject forever!"

Donovan sat down; tears were on his cheeks.

After a brief space of silence Trelawney reached out of the prisoner's box and pressed his hand in gratitude.

The attorney for the state arose, and after commenting severely on the address of Col. Donovan, began to discuss the circumstantial evidence that had been brought out in the trial.

His face wore a smile of triumph peculiar to prosecutors everywhere, when sure of their cases. In a short time, however, he paused, saying: "The evidence as presented to you in this case, gentlemen of the jury, is all conclusive of the guilt of these prisoners, and I shall not longer tax your patience or the patience of the honorable court in discussing it; it would be an insult to your intelligence—so I shall rest here."

Then after a stern, brief charge from the court, which in its general tenor seemed to be much against the accused men, the jury retired.

IV.

Two hours later the ringing of the court house bell announced to the citizens that the jury was ready to render its verdict.

All the waiting crowd hastened to the seat of justice, the attorneys assembled, and the prisoners were brought into the dim light of that dingy old room, there to await their fate.

It was more than half an hour before the court could be found, and the suspense must have been very trying to the prisoners, as it was evidently to the jurors who appeared ill at ease under the calm gaze of the two men whose *all* was in their hands.

When the court appeared and the usual formula had been propounded, the foreman of the jury arose and said in a weak and trembling voice:

"We, the jury, find John Symonds and James Trelawney, the prisoners at the bar, guilty of murder in the first degree!"

Then silence fell on the room, which was broken only when the judge ordered the prisoners to be returned to their cells.

This verdict was a foregone conclusion; it called forth no expression of surprise or of pity for the condemned men.

Three days after this time the prisoners were arraigned before the court in order to receive their sentence.

"Stand up!" said the judge to the prisoners.

They both arose and stood in soldierly attitude, Symonds taking his place a little to the rear of Trelawney.

"What have you to say, John Symonds, why the court should not now proceed to pass sentence upon you according to law?" demanded the judge with unusual severity.

Symonds cast a quick glance at Trelawney as if seeking aid, but the latter did not remove his eyes from the court. Then the prisoner looked helplessly to the bench and shook his head in stolid despair, remaining silent.

When the court turned to Trelawney with the same query he had made the other, this prisoner raised his hand, as if in military salute, and spoke with grave dignity as follows:

"I have nothing, your Honor, to say, that can

change this verdict; I merely raise my voice to protest my innocence, and the innocence of my companion. I think our innocence may be proven within the lifetime of some now here present; if not, it will be proven in the world to come!

"I will admit that it is a grievous thing for me, who have always lived an honorable life, to die an ignominious death; but I shall try to bear my last burden here, as I have borne misfortune in other lands."

He then bowed to the court in token that he had finished.

The judge without following the usual preamble, said: "James Trelawney and John Symonds, the sentence of this court is that you, and each of you, shall on the third Friday in December next, between the hours of 10 a. m. and 3 p. m., be taken to the place of execution, and there hanged by the neck until you are both dead, dead!

"May God have mercy on your souls!

"Sheriff, return the prisoners to their cells."

The crowd dispersed, discussing as they went out the merits of the trial. But one who spoke in a loud voice seemed to express the sentiment of all, when he exclaimed:

"These land pirates won't come in here again and kill one of our best citizens!"

"Oh no," said another, "they'll stay here till Gabriel blows his horn!"

And this poor wit evoked laughter from the

vengeful crew, who rejoiced in anticipation of "a hanging," a rare spectacle for them, and more in their thoughts than any triumph of justice.

The few remaining weeks were occupied by the condemned men in making appropriate preparations for their end. But they continued to observe unusual reticence in regard to their past lives; they claimed that their past had nothing to do with their present forlorn condition.

However, it was learned from the meager details let fall at different times, that Trelawney, though English by birth, had served for many years in some army of Asia, and that Symonds had been his military servant.

After the trial the effects of Trelawney had been returned to him by order of the court. It was found that he possessed eight or ten thousand pounds in English money besides papers or memoranda concerning property in England.

He wrote his will with his own hand, leaving his money and property to his nephew, one Edward Trewlaney, with the English army in Europe; at least, he was supposed to be there. He sent as a precaution a letter directed to the Club frequented by his nephew when in London.

His best horse he presented to Col. Donovan, "his respected friend;" the other, he gave to Luttrell, "in remembrance of the last day's sport he ever had on earth!"

He also rewarded liberally the few persons
who had shown him any kindness or had be-
friended him in any way. In concluding his
last will and testament, he made only one request; but that was a very singular one, indeed!

It ran as follows: "I earnestly beseech those
in charge to permit my body, after execution,
to remain in the open air for the period of two
days before interment. And may it be meted to
you, in your last extremity, as you shall heed
this prayer of a dying man!"

There was no one to claim the remains of this
doomed man, and as the sheriff had profited
much by his generosity, he consented to this
proposition, strange and weird as it was, and
promised faithfully to carry out his wishes.

The execution was to take place not far from
the Taggart House, and "the platform of the
scaffold," said the sheriff, "could be removed
and placed under the portico of that ancient
house, and on this, the body could remain in the
open air for two days under the care of a watchman."

For this service a liberal sum of money was
appropriated. The fatal day of execution at last
arrived, as all days come, whether freighted
with joy or sorrow. However, there is not much
to be told about it except to relate in detail the
dark and mysterious occurrences which grew
out of this last and singular request of Trelawney.

The day was bright and beautiful as ever shone in December. Col. Donovan and Luttrell were early at the prison to bid farewell to their friends, as they were not to be present at the execution. The colonel called it "a legal murder," and was very much downcast. But Trelawney himself cheered Donovan up in a hearty fashion, saying: "Colonel, you have done all you could for me; there is nothing with which to blame yourself; go on and enjoy your life—may heaven bless you! Farewell, my friend!"

Then for a moment he gazed through the open door and his eyes marked the blue hills that lined the distant horizon; turning to Luttrell he slapped him on the shoulder and said: "This would be a fine day for a chase, old man! Good-bye, a long farewell!"

The friends then parted to meet no more.

There was a great concourse of people about the gallows; it was expected that Trelawney would address the people, and perhaps relate the adventures of his life, as the public curiosity was much aroused by this interesting and mysterious character.

If such was the general expectation, the people were doomed to disappointment, for he spoke not one word.

It should be noted, however, that by this time, after the fates of these men had been sealed irrevocably, there was something of a revulsion of public sentiment in regard to their guilt and there were those present who began to doubt the justness of the sentence that had doomed them to death.

As they mounted the scaffold their foreign, semi-military dress, and especially the distinguished bearing of Trelawney, was remarked by the vast multitude of people who had thronged to the execution as to a show.

Trelawney stood calmly viewing the landscape while the last preparations were making; Symonds, who stood at his left side, seemed to take his cue from him as if content to follow where he might lead.

In conclusion, the sheriff asked them if they were ready; the elder man bowed; the other bowed, like an automaton; the drop fell, and these two souls passed from earth away.

V.

A few hours after the people had dispersed, the sheriff took away the remains of Symonds for burial; but the body of Trelawney, according to his promise, he placed on the platform, under the portico of the old Taggart house.

And here, in his easy chair, with his blankets wrapped about him, old Tom Slaton, a character of the town, took his station to watch through the night. He was armed with his pipe and a half pint of whisky, and thought he could easily earn ten dollars, as it was pretty certain that no one of the vicinity would disturb his vigils in that ghostly place.

By eleven o'clock Tom Slaton was sleeping the sleep that is usually supposed to belong to the just, but which also appertains to the intemperate; and when he awoke from his slumber it was not only daylight, but the sun was shining full on the eastern end of the portico.

"It's all right," he said, "there's no one in sight, and no doubt the dead man is resting comfortably on the platform up there."

But he didn't go to look, not he. "I'll wait till the sheriff comes," he said.

It was nine o'clock when the sheriff came. He and Slaton then climbed up to the level of the platform, so as to view the remains. They little expected the surprise that awaited them.

For when their heads reached high enough, they saw absolutely nothing. The body of Trelawney had vanished, but whether into the earth or sky, there was no trace left behind to show.

This was incomprehensible, and the sheriff stood dumbfounded. Soon, however, a large number of people collected about the place; and Slaton, mounted upon a chair, began to discourse to them in an excited manner.

"I never closed my eyes during the whole night," he said. "This act of vandalism must have been perpetrated by the accursed ghosts. I heard them marching up and down stairs here in this old house all night. By the Lord, it fairly made my hair raise on my head!"

This last assertion would, perhaps, have provoked a laugh, as Slaton was bald, but they were all too much frightened for that.

The more thoughtful citizens held to the belief that the remains had been taken away by surgeons for the purpose of dissection and that they must certainly be concealed somewhere nearby. A "tracking snow" had fallen early the preceding night, and there was not the slightest trace or trail leading from the portico.

Every part of the town was searched, and especially every nook and corner in the old Taggart house, without discovering the slightest clew to the mystery.

The excitement was unabated not only on that day but for many days thereafter. For there was yet to happen in connection with this sad affair an event which would increase the consternation of the citizens, and would be the theme of many a tale in the years to come.

Although there was nothing to watch, it was thought best in view of the mysterious circumstances, that Slaton should take his place the second night on the old portico and there await developments.

Slaton came the second night better fortified

against ghosts than before; at least, he was better supplied with whiskey, and by half past ten o'clock he was safe in the lap of Morpheus. He awoke as before after daylight, and thought all was well, as fears of ghosts and evil spirits always vanish with the sunshine.

When the sheriff came, he and Slaton, prompted by some unknown impulse, proceeded again to look on the platform; the sight they there beheld filled them with fear and amazement.

For there lay the body of Trelawney, booted and spurred and splashed with mud, as if it had just dismounted from his horse!

No words can express the consternation of the spectators who soon gathered around. Slaton declared solemnly: "I never slept a wink last night, but walked this portico the whole night through; I saw nobody, and I didn't hear anything except the ghosts galloping round in this old Taggart house that every body knows is haunted!"

"I oughtn't be held responsible for what the infernal ghosts have done! The sheriff has got Trelawney all safe here now, and my advice is, that he take him and bury him at once before he has any more trouble with him—them's my sentiments!"

This was considered good advice, and the remains of Trelawney were placed in the grave.

The astounding news of the return of the

body of Trelawney to the scaffold had only added fuel to the flame of excitement which was all aglow in the breasts of these terrified citizens. And in their endeavor to explain the inexplicable, and to account in reason for the irrational, there were many diverse theories advanced.

One was that Slaton had fallen asleep and that all this fiendish work was but the cruel jest of some lunatic or frantic fool, who had just escaped from a bedlam. But as there were no lunatic asylums in this vicinity and as there were none of the neighborhood known to be entirely bereft of reason, this theory was not generally accepted.

When a deputation of citizens waited on Col. Donovan and questioned him in regard to these mysteries, the old lawyer said:

"I wash my hands of this whole matter; all I know about it is that two innocent men have been executed, and if it is possible for the spirits of injured men to return from the other world to torment those who have persecuted them, I think this is a proper place and a proper occasion for such demoniacal exhibitions!"

There was not much of comfort for any citizen in these words or in the event that had influenced their utterance; and many sleepless hours were passed by those who pondered on these strange and mysterious happenings.

Not long after the execution of Trelawney and Symonds, the public offices were removed to the new court house and the old Taggart house remained tenantless for nearly three years. Then the new Presbyterian minister, Rev. Mr. Henry, and his wife moved into it. They remained here for nearly fourteen years until the reverend gentleman retired from the ministry and returned to the home of his youth. During all these years the minister and his wife were never heard to utter a word about the ghosts that were known to frequent their house.

The first year of their sojourn here, this subject was occasionally broached in their presence; but this soon ceased, when it was found to irritate the minister, and to call forth, always, a reply pointed with the keenest sarcasm.

As the years fled, the careworn countenance of Mrs. Henry was attributed by her neighbors to the annoyances of the evil spirits that abode beneath her ill-omened roof! Yet there was some compensation at least in a residence here, for Mrs. Henry could raise the fattest turkeys and chickens and they could roost on the lowest trees in her yard unmolested, for no matter how hard the season or how urgent the necessity, no prowler of the night would intrude on these premises.

And now the old minister and his family had gone away and the old Taggart house was once more tenantless and presented a very forlorn and forbidding appearance.

It was about this time that the clerk of the county court received from the West a legal document that was to revive with added horror the tragic events related of Trelawney.

This paper was in the form of a declaration made in *articulo mortis*, and was subscribed to by one Absalom Meeks.

Meeks, believing himself to be on his death-bed, stated:

"I, Absalom Meeks, wish to make this my solemn statement in the face of death, that justice may be done. Job Archer, now deceased, and myself were traveling from Richmond, Va., in the year 1826, to our homes on the Ohio River in that state. This was in the month of October, and as we were on our journey we overtook, in Staunton, ex-sheriff Hinton of the town of Clonmel, and sheriff Hinton told us then that he would reach his home on the following Friday night. Now we had found out while we were in Richmond that he would carry to his home a large sum of money from that city. And while Archer and myself were traveling on foot, two days ahead of Hinton, we often talked about his bringing the money. We reached the stable of one Luttrell, a few miles from Clonmel, on that Friday night after dark. We found in the stable two horses with saddles and bridles and pistols.

We rested here for some time, when Archer proposed that we should take the horses; this we did and then rode on until we reached a dark, narrow place in the road. Here we stopped for the purpose of robbing Hinton. We knew he would come along pretty soon. After a time he did come and in the excitement we shot and killed him, although we only meant to rob him. Archer said that now we would be followed and that we had better take the horses and pistols back to the stable, where we got them, and go home through the woods. This we did, and after we reached our homes on the Ohio river we thought we would be found out. So we moved to Pike County, Missouri, where Job Archer died last year and where this paper is written. In conclusion, I, Absalom Meeks, believing this to be my dying declaration, do solemnly swear that these statements are true and nothing but the truth, as I hope for mercy."

This informal declaration was attested by one Dr. Jerrold, and the minister in attendance, the Rev. Simon Felton. It also bore the seal of Pike County, Missouri, and the affidavit of the clerk of the county court, to the effect that Absalom Meeks had died the day after signing the declaration.

Thus it became known to the citizens of Clonmel that in their town twenty years before, two innocent men had died on the gallows.

It was well enough before these facts were confirmed that old Col. Donovan was sleeping in his grave. Luttrell too, had passed away, but there were living yet, those who had witnessed the trial and execution of James Trelawney and John Symonds.

The strange story of these men burdened with irreparable wrong, then became the subject of common conversation. Men told of the frightful happenings at the Taggart house in connection with the execution of Trelawney. And Tom Slaton, the eye-witness to these occurrences, was still here and ready to speak for himself.

The words of Col. Donavan were recalled, and the speech of Trelawney, when he had proclaimed in open court: "I think our innocence may be proven even within the lifetime of some now here present!"

"And were they not present and alive to testify that Trelawney spoke the truth?"

"But what was the good of it; he was dead!"

"I am not so sure of that," said Tom Slaton, "for I have seen things—strange things—that I don't care to talk about to young people!"

Well, there was no reparation to make and the sad knowledge that two innocent men had been executed in that town, only added to the burden and care of a few elderly citizens, who now deplored the hasty trial and the short shrift that had been accorded the ill-fated strangers.

VI.

From its connection with these sad affairs, the evil name of the old Taggart house, now kept as a tavern by one Mark Tudor, became darker than ever. Yet it was tolerably well patronized by the emigrants who passed this way to the western country. However, it was noticeable that the citizens of the town were rarely seen there after nightfall.

Now, when the discussion of the dying declaration of Meeks brought to mind all the mysterious bedevilment that had followed the execution, the landlord began to have much trouble with his servants. For the disappearance and the re-appearance of the body of Trelawney could never be explained by those who related the story as the great mystery of the "haunted house."

And now that it was know that Trelawney had died an innocent man, it was not to be presumed that he would lie quietly in his grave; but that he would "revisit at times, the glimpses of the moon," so that living men might not forget his wrongs!

At least this was the philosophy of Tom Slaton and several of the older citizens, who knew the most about the execution.

It was about this time that spiritualism had its rise in this country; and the "rappings" and such disturbances, accompanied by apparitions—

which no rational beings could explain—fully
re-established the time-honored belief in "haunted
houses," that a realistic age had almost dispelled.

A number of lecturers on spiritualism had
held "seances" in the old Taggart house, and they
admitted with one accord that it was the very
headquarters of all the spirits. As for "rappings" and "table-tippings"—they were common
affairs and most any of the lecturers could "call
up" the spirit of Trelawney; his jingling spurs
could be heard as he marched with stately step
up and down the old stairway!

But it was the most troublesome thing in the
world to have him appear at times when he was
not "called up," and when no one wanted to see
him.

In fact, things went from bad to worse at this
"haunted tavern," and what with the groans in
the garret, and with Trelawney marching around
every night—most of the guests were driven
from the house, and the servants fled incontin-
ently!

It was the day after the servants had left, that
Tom Slaton was walking past the Taggart house,
and when nearly opposite to it, he became all at
once very deeply interested in the appearance of
a stranger, who was walking to and fro on the
portico.

Slaton looked at this man first with his right
and then with his left eye; turning his head the

while, after the manner of a turkey. He then took off his hat and ran down the road as fast as he could go; and did not stop till he arrived at the house of the old ex-sheriff, William Finch. Here, he sat down on a bench by the door, but it was some time before he could speak. As soon as he was able he called for Finch, and when he appeared, said: "Bill, didn't you hang Trelawney over there by the Taggart House, twenty years ago?"

Finch looked at Slaton curiously, and replied very slowly: "You know I did, and I am very sorry for it now, too."

"Well, Bill, he's over there now, walking up and down the old portico! I saw him with my two eyes, and it's a sight I never expected to see in broad daylight!" was the rejoinder of Slaton.

To this astounding statement, after a long silence, Finch replied: "Slaton I have heard enough of these ghosts stories; now, if Trelawney is over there and alive, I want to see him!"

Through much persuasion Slaton was induced to return, and being joined by another old citizen, the trio soon arrived in front of the Taggart House tavern.

Now, as they were approaching they noticed Tudor, the landlord, in conversation with the stranger, but as he passed on into the house, Slaton observed: "That don't count, Tudor didn't know him before he was hung!"

When they got near enough to see distinctly, Finch became more excited, if anything, than Slaton had been; he exclaimed:

"Great heavens, that is Trelawney, sure enough!"

And while they stood there unable to move through fear, Trelawney stopped, and taking his cigar from his mouth, called out:

"Hello, Tom Slaton, is that you? How are you, Finch?"

This was more than their nerves could bear, and the trio hastily took their departure without standing on the order of it.

Soon the whole town was in a furor of excitement, and Slaton swore that he would never go near that haunted place again, if he lived to be a hundred!

The next morning a number of citizens went over to interview Tudor. He said: "The stranger, who appeared to be a very fine man, had come there the evening before, and had left that morning on the stage coach."

"His name? oh, yes, there it is on the register."

And there, sure enough, they found, written in a bold hand, the signature—"Trelawney, London, England!"

The sight of this name appeared to cast a spell on these excited citizens, so that they left the tavern hastily, shaking their heads, but asking no more questions.

However, Tudor had not taken the trouble to inform his anxious enquirers that he had prompted the stranger in regard to the names of Slaton and Finch, when those two cronies appeared to be taking such a deep interest in his (the stranger's) appearance.

So that when Tudor sought to explain these matters later, it was all taken as an afterthought, and his neighbors presumed he was only trying to bolster up the failing credit of his tavern.

But things were continually growing worse, and had been tending that way for several years at this old mansion; so that Tudor was, perforce, induced to listen to the proposition of the Rev. Slaton-Hicks, who said: "I shall come over some evening, about sundown, with a few of my steadiest church people, and hold a short, religious service on that old portico; after which, I shall lecture the people on the folly and sinfulness of a belief in ghosts, and I think that will surely quiet things."

Now, the Rev. Slaton-Hicks was a very learned young man; he was not only deeply versed in the scriptures, but he also knew a great deal about Latin and Greek and many other things; moreover, he was a nephew of our old friend, Slaton, and one of whom he was very proud.

On this occasion Slaton remarked: "I would have gone anywhere else in the whole world to have heard my nephew preach, except to the Taggart house; but not there, I beg to be excused!"

William Finch, when he heard of this proposed meeting, said: "Maybe the Rev. Slaton-Hicks knows a great deal about ghosts; but I would consider him a very great man, if he could tell me how Trelawney, after I had hung him until dead and placed his body on the Taggart House portico—how that body went away and came back again, twenty-four hours later! And how that body went away with shoes on, and came back again wearing boots and spurs! Oh, yes! it's all very well to talk, but how did Trelawney come back and walk on that portico, and call Slaton and myself by name, twenty years after he had been hung? If there are no spirits, how can such things be? Now, if the Rev. Slaton-Hicks will explain these things to me, I will be willing to throw in the 'rappings' and the 'table tippings,' as matters of no consequence!"

On the evening appointed for the lecture there was a large crowd assembled at the old mansion; there were even many boys, but the latter stood out in the road, so that if anything did happen, they might not be embarrassed by gates and fences but, as they said: "We will have a fair show to get away."

Everything went off very well during the short religious exercises except noises were heard in the upper part of the house which sounded like moans or groans. "That is the cooing of pigeons in the attic," Tudor said; but as there were no pigeons seen flying around the place, some persons shook their heads, in distrust; however, the explanation was generally accepted.

The Rev. Slaton-Hicks made a very "beautiful lecture" as the ladies said: the force of it was directed principally against spiritualism, "that modern skepticism which has revived all the ghostly superstitions of the Mediæval ages," as he defined it.

And he was going on in this strain in a very fine fashion, when the boys in the road became vociferous and began to move off at a pretty lively pace.

This desire to get away seemed to possess those on the eastern end of the portico also, and the crowd there thinned out rapidly, which enabled the Rev. Slaton-Hicks to see as far as the pump that stood on that side of the yard. His eyes were fixed on that homely object, but more especially on the pump-handle, which they all now observed was working violently up and down, without any living soul being near it, to cause the motion!

"Gentlemen, this is incomprehensible!" exclaimed the Rev. Slaton-Hicks as he gazed at the preternatural exhibition. "I can't explain that!"

But by this time most of the people had left the portico and were making their way towards the town, and the farther they went the faster they went.

Yet, when they arrived at the court house, the Rev. Slaton-Hicks was not the hindmost one by any means!

Here, a number of persons stopped at the court house gate, and among them were Tudor and his family.

"It's no use denying it any longer," said Tudor, "the ghosts or spirits surely have possession of that old house, and if I live till to-morrow, I shall move out of it, and have nothing more to do with it forever."

On the very next day the Taggart house became tenantless, and its ancient halls and rooms were destined never again to resound to pleasant human voices.

VII.

It is singular to note that most of the old citizens had passed away, and the plowshare had furrowed the site on which the Taggart mansion had stood, when its dark impenetrable mysteries were unfolded in a distant city.

Guy Donovan, the son of the old colonel, had always taken a deep interest in the story of the unhappy Trelawney. And so, when on a business trip to New York, he had learned that

Edward Trelawney, the nephew of James Trelawney, and the legatee of his will was at that time in the city—he called to see him.

Donovan was astonished to observe the remarkable likeness that this man bore to his uncle; he, whose perturbed spirit was the supposed cause of all the preternatural occurrences that had afflicted the citizens of his native town.

Edward Trelawny informed him that he had learned through his legal adviser, who had secured his bequest for him, all the particulars concerning the trial and the untimely death of his uncle.

"I have received." he said, "from the same source a copy of the dying statement of Absalom Meeks, which has substantiated the innocence of my uncle.

"I was traveling through the western country," he continued, "when curiosity led me to stop at the town which had been the scene of my uncle's misfortunes.

"I was even entertained at the tavern that had been so intimately connected with the last days in the life drama of my gallant, but unfortunate kinsman.

"While there, I remember very distinctly to have called out to the men you have named; they appeared to be taking a great interest in my appearance on that porch, and as I thought I could divine the cause, I hailed them, when the landlord had given me their names. I regret now very much that I did so. I had no idea that the effect of that little adventure would be so great or so enduring."

"And this," exclaimed Donovan, "is the simple explanation of the great mystery, that not only bewildered and frightened Slaton and Finch but the whole neighborhood!"

It was destined that Donovan, while in New York, was to be instrumental in solving another great mystery. He met there Dr. Cool, an old physician and surgeon, who had formerly lived in the town of Winston, about twenty miles from C. Now, in conversation with Dr. Cool, Donovan had related to him his interview with Edward Trelawney and the revelations the latter had made.

Thereupon, Dr. Cool said, it was about time that he himself should make an explanation or an apology.

"I was a young, practicing surgeon in the town of Winston," he stated, "when Trelawney was executed at C.

"At that time it was extremely difficult for surgeons to procure subjects for dissection. As I then had two medical students studying under my instruction, and was very anxious to obtain the body of one of the men who were to be executed at C., I repaired to that place. But I found upon my arrival that the condemned men had ample means to defray all their expenses, and so I was at a loss to know how I could accomplish my purpose.

"The common prejudice against exhumation for such a purpose, was at that time very strong indeed, and surgeons were compelled to act with great precaution in procuring subjects.

"But after I had learned of the singular circumstance, that the body of one of the men was to remain in the air for two days after the execution, I began to think this body might be procured. As it happened, a brother of one of my medical students was a writer in the clerk's office at Clonmel, which office, as you remember, was located in an old private residence.

"To this young man, under a charge of great secrecy, I divulged the object of my visit to his town; and in behalf of his brother's interest, I begged for his assistance.

"This he consented to render, and the day before the execution he showed me a little closet, or secret room, which he had accidentally discovered in the wall of the clerk's office.

"This secret room was about three feet by eight feet, and was entered by means of a movable panel in the wainscoting of the old room. The young man had not shown his discovery to any one besides myself, and when we found that the remains of the executed man were to rest for two days prior to interment on the portico of the old house, and within a few feet of the clerk's office, and the secret chamber, it occurred to us that it would be practicable to remove and conceal them in that secret place, until I could find opportunity to convey the cadaver to my office in Winston, twenty miles distant.

"So the night of the execution we concealed ourselves in the clerk's office, and after the watchman on the porch had fallen asleep we stole from our place of hiding, and removing the remains, hid them in the secret chamber. We then fastened the panel, so that it would not slide back, and piled law papers and books against it, nearly up to the ceiling.

"As a deep snow fell that night after dark, we were afraid to leave the court house on account of the tracks we should make. Therefore, we concealed ourselves again in the office. But in the morning, when the news of the disappearance of the remains had caused a large crowd of excited people to gather around, we slipped out and mingled with them.

"As you know, the excitement grew as the day advanced, and the whole town was diligently searched. But we had no fears of the discovery of our secret room, at least not for two or three days, when of course, natural causes would have led to its detection. But I soon found I was very strongly suspected, being known to many of the citizens as a surgeon and an instructor of

medical students.　This in addition to the condition of the weather, caused me to fear that I
should not be able to transfer the remains from
their hiding place to my office in Winston, without detection.

"During the course of the day I held several
brief consultations with my young friend, the
clerk, and expressed to him my fears.　We had
not counted on the people being so greatly excited, nor on being so closely watched ourselves.
The clerk said some of the citizens looked on the
disappearance of the body as a thing miraculous,
as there was not left behind the vestige of a trace,
and the remains were known to have been on the
portico after the snow had ceased to fall.

"Finally, after I decided to return the remains
to the platform, whence I had taken them, this
knowledge of a belief in the supernatural on the
part of the citizens, induced the young clerk to
perform an act which I did not entirely ap-
prove.

"By some means he had obtained possession
of the dead man's spurs, and these he adjusted
to the boots of the corpse, and then mixed a little mud with melted snow and splashed the
clothing, after we had placed the body exactly
as we had found it on the platform.　"This,' he
said, 'will add to the mystery, and turn suspicion from you, Doctor."

"It certainly had the first effect!" exclaimed

the doctor. "We had pursued the same tactics as before," he continued; "that is, we had concealed ourselves in the clerk's office, but we were surprised to see the old watchman on the porch the second night, as there was nothing to watch. He gave us little trouble, however, as he was soon fast asleep. We were very particular in arranging the remains as they had been, and it was impossible for any one to notice the slightest difference in their disposal, with the exception of the spurs and the splashings of the mud Now, as luck would have it, the snow had fallen again in the early morning and then ceased. Hence, we were compelled to hide in the building till daylight for the same reason as before.

"So, when the sheriff came, there was not a track about the house, but there was the body of the dead man, after an absence of twenty-four hours, booted and splashed with mud, as if just returned from a journey."

This was the story that Dr. Cool recounted to Guy Donovan in New York. And when he had finished, Donovan cried: "Doctor, you have solved the great mystery that has perplexed the people of our town for more than twenty years."

The strange phenomenon of the pump was also brought to light about this time.

It appears that a few days prior to the lecture given on the portico of the Taggart house by Rev. Slaton-Hicks, two young miners were dig-

ging coal on the lands adjoining the Taggart
manor, and whilst they knew they were trespas-
sing on the latter, they were not aware that they
were so nearly under the house, until one day in
digging, they cut a hole in the pump-stock with
their picks. They were alarmed, lest their tres-
pass should be discovered; so they sawed out a
piece from the broken stock, and neatly fitted a
block of wood therein, so that the stock might not
be taken up for repairs, and thus reveal their mine
under the Taggart lands.

Now these two miners were present at the services held by the Rev. Slaton-Hicks, and the
thought occurred to one of them that by going
down into the mine, he could by taking out the
block from the stock, work the pump-handle by
taking hold of the rod, and thus add his quota
to the ghost business.

Now, when the pump-handle began to move
by the unseen hand, there was only one man in
the large crowd, gathered about the old portico,
who understood what it all meant, and his lips
were sealed for the reasons given.

The explanation of all this was brought about,
when the miners on the Taggart lands also ran
their "heading" against the pump-stock, when
the "workings" of the other miners were disclosed, and the neatly fitted block of wood in the
pump-stock, explained the last mystery of "the
old haunted house.

Time assuages sorrow and allays excitement, but it brings no compensation for irretrievable mistakes; and many marvel now at the blind zeal of their fathers in pursuing, on the trail laid by artifice, innocent men to their doom. But this trail, "circumstantial evidence," will never again lead to death in the courts of Clonmel, until the events here narrated have faded from memory.

THE END.